REAR GUARD

REAR GUARD

JAMES WARNER BELLAH

CUTTING EDGE

ISBN-13: 978-1-954840-64-5

Published by
Cutting Edge Books
PO Box 8212
Calabasas, CA 91372
www.cuttingedgebooks.com

For
"HUGHIE" MATHEWS
Lieutenant Colonel, United States Army
KILLED ON OMAHA
EASY RED

*A friend, a gay companion, a good officer
and as splendid an example of a fighting
man as you will find on the rolls of his
beloved West Point*

CHAPTER ONE

D TROOP lost two hours of its sixteen-day forced march because Doctor MacLaw had to open Lieutenant Forsythe's abdomen to get the head of the arrow loose. He got it, but it wasn't going to be any good, and MacLaw knew it, and Forsythe knew it. First Sergeant Elliott knew it, and a rat-gnaw of worry began within him, for without an officer in command something of confidence went out of the Sergeant and a miserable, piddling uncertainty took its place. That had always been the way with Sergeant Elliott—a good detail man only if responsibility were not upon his shoulders.

The blankets, with the waterproof operating sheet, were spread by the trail side, with a small fire for boiling the doctor's water. The fire was guttering to white ash for lack of fuel now and the thick scarf of its smoke trailed low over the line of saddles. A horse nearby whinnied on the picket rope, and a trooper called softly, "Shut up, Sal; you talk too much." Mr. Forsythe was not a young man any more, and the Army had not been too generous to him. For beans on Saturday night and one silver bar, it had taken twenty-two hard years from Forsythe and the accounts were closing. "Forsythe, R.G., 1st Lieut.—from Duty to Died of Wounds" —for he kept his command function, in spite of his agony, until the moment he died.

There wasn't much left in Forsythe, to struggle against it— after two days in an escort wagon with white flame inside him, and no very overpowering regrets—for his contract with the United States was too old a habit of his mind. He lay there, alive

1

only in his eyes, now that the mountain air had cleared the chloroform from his brain.

Everything he had come from was gone in the mists of the years he had spent with U.S. on his saddle blanket. Long since, his parents were dead in the comfortable house on Utica Street, with the gate that had creaked to his schoolboy hand. So long since that he had been unable to conjure up their faces for many years, only the faint smell of sandalwood and lavender water that had been his mother, and the great gold watch and chain that was all he could remember of his father. His sister Agatha had always been faintly uncomfortable in her proper soul that he had gone into the Army instead of the marts of trade. It didn't seem steady to Agatha, or quite decent, to have one's mailing address shift eternally all over the face of the West and never to quite know where a member of the family was at any given time or what he was doing. So from letters, she had tapered off to only a card at Christmas and for the last several years not even that. It is amazing what little residue of his living a man can leave in this world. A world of nostalgia in a forgotten letter. The memory of his smile in youth in the heart of some woman, long since gone her way with someone else. One man to say, "Ray Forsythe was a great guy, but you had to get to know him." For the rest—worn clothing, a few dog-eared books, a Castellani sabre, two hand guns and four hundred fifteen dollars and thirty cents and the account of forty-three years of living is closed.

Doctor MacLaw was a lean man of the Antrim blood. When he failed at his trade of surgery, a wire-thonged anger flayed his soul. It must have shown in his face because Forsythe said, "It's all right, Doc. I knew it when I was hit," and he also said, "Sergeant Elliott, the doctor has served with this Regiment off and on for many years; he's back with us again for this campaign, with the rank of captain. You're a crack top soldier but you are no troop commander, Elliott. Dr. MacLaw will command the troop, then, until it rejoins the Regiment at Fort Starke. That's an order—and Army Regulations be damned."

MacLaw knelt with his own gentle hands on Forsythe's, as he had so many times before, while Death came in from the scrub oak and scuttled through the bivouac.

Sergeant Elliott put his hat back on his head and faced the doctor. A hardheaded man, Elliott, with the years of his own service lived in the safe runway of duty. With the course to be traveled prescribed in minute detail, and nothing to right or to left of it, but punishment for infraction. That way, he had come to his stripes. That way, he had never lost a stripe or a day's pay. That way, he had never been under the command of a doctor, and the thought was faint trouble in his eyes. "Yes, sir?" he said. "Orders, Sir?"

Dr. MacLaw stood for a moment, looking absently at the gunstock brown of the Sergeant's face, but his mind wasn't seeing it. His mind was far in the future of surgery, when some man, thinking well beyond his time and beyond the books, would discover something to do about multiple perforations of the ilium.

The sergeant felt a slight, embarrassed discomfort under the doctor's gaze, for the doctor looked like a cavalry officer. Long in the leg, thin-waisted below a good chest, with his eyes bleached pale by the Western distances. But there was the book, between them—and something more than the book—that surgical operation. As Elliott had watched it, it had been a thing of fine ritual. Almost a religious service at an altar, that had taken Elliott back in his mind to his believing days, that had lifted the doctor beyond the mortality of D Troop to the minor godhood which is the cloak of fine surgery.

MacLaw smiled pleasantly. It was an old trick. When you first came into the sickroom, catch the patient's eye and smile impersonally and dismiss the disease in the quick humanity of meeting. He could classify Elliott now, far better than Forsythe had classified him, for the doctor always searched back into childhood when he looked into a man's eyes. Men enlist in the standing army for any number of reasons of last resort. Hunger, failure elsewhere, anonymity, impending winter, or an instinct for suicide without the full madness to accomplish it alone. One in a hundred wants to be a soldier. But whatever they enlist for, they get, for it is the school of last resort and it has seldom failed to pay individual debts through the magnificence of team performance. Sergeant Elliott had come in for his manhood. Deep in his eyes there was the timidity of insecurity—a boy kicked from pillar to post without the inner virus to become potent by harassment. With no strength himself outside the system. So he had taken the system gratefully, conformed to it, risen through it until the splints of it sustained him fully. In conformity, he could act. In full responsibility, he would always fail, for he had no ability to splint himself.

"Yes," MacLaw said. "Orders. Saddle and mount the troop, sergeant. Prepare to move out. We'll bury Mr. Forsythe at Cashman's tonight." Then he said, "And, Sergeant Elliott, don't worry," and he smiled, and embarrassment left the Sergeant.

At the foot of the rise before the last ridge line that masked the river fork and hid the town of Cashman's in the valley below, MacLaw said, "Halt the troop, sergeant, and dismount and breathe the horses for ten minutes, before we start to climb. No watering."

Something rather fine clicked inside Sergeant Elliott's skull and he felt good all over, for that is the way to treat horses. And he thought comfortably, *This is going to work out all right. Seven more days and we'll rejoin the regiment and get a new officer, and seven days is easy, even with a doctor in command.*

The doctor had them walk up the rise, leading the mounts, and he was first over the crest—first to see the infantry regiment camped in the river fork below. Twelve company streets, white walled in canvas, surveyed evenly on lines of bayonets, latrined and wagon-parked and clean, with officers' row along North Branch and a stand of colors in front of the Old Man's tent.

"Regulars, sir," Elliott said.

Doctor MacLaw nodded.

Sergeant Elliott said, "Sir, behind you, about eleven miles straightaway across the Estrellas"—and he pointed—"that's Indian smoke, sir."

MacLaw turned and looked at the distant puffed wisp from the hilltop. He said, "Yes. They must be paralleling our march, sergeant. That fight we had two days ago when Mr. Forsythe was hit, and now here. I dare say all the tribes are off their reservations to rally round Sitting Bull, don't you?" He turned again and jerked his head toward the regiment encamped below. "Have the men take off their shirts and beat the dust out of them. Sleeves rolled down and hats cocked over their eyes. Uncover the guidon and fly it. Mount," the doctor said. "Twos. Twos right. At the walk." But down in the flatlands below, the doctor called Waller the trumpeter to him and he said, "We'll break trumpet silence, trumpeter, and go in on the horn. Sound the Trot and put spit into it," and that way D Troop came to town, for a walking regiment to see them arrive.

CHAPTER TWO

CASHMAN'S is two streets at right angles. Twenty houses in all, with the telegraphic office and the coach station and two abandoned threads of rusted track that lead on back east to Ferguson, where the main railroad line goes south. And that ends Cashman's, except that this time when MacLaw saw it the place was full of prairie schooners, and women and quite a few children and civilian men. An emigrant convoy.

You could feel the men tighten up in their guts at sight of the women, casing the setup for hook shops and crib wagons. The tension ran through the troop like a drawn wire. How long had this doughfoot outfit been organizing the terrain, breaking down the fences, sleeping with their shirts off? Their eyes were hungry, and they came up in their saddles, but there wasn't a woman that looked like a yellow ribbon, so they took it out on jawbone shack-ups with the pretty ones, looking them over, dry run, as they rode past and figuring how soon they could get the housekeeping done in the bivouac and get free to rope out a stray for record. Because there's always a stray. Sometimes you can spot her a mile. Sometimes it takes time, and the last thing a troop on the march has is time. So if they're big enough, they're old enough and good bye, good luck and hope he makes corporal when he grows up.

There was the memory in Doctor MacLaw of a young wife, dead in the years behind him. And in some men that makes for filling with work all the hours of wakefulness beyond the working hours, for there is no one left to go home to at sundown. He didn't brood—the doctor—but at times in towns, he searched unconsciously from his loneliness, for a girl's straight shoulders, carried so. For the whip of a skirt. For a head held high and the flash of a smile. And suddenly, there it all was, just for a tiny second, in a tall girl who passed quickly between two of the wagons, the better to see D Troop. A girl with white teeth and a hand to brush back a wisp of tawny hair, and a quick, excited smile at the sight of mounted soldiery.

It wasn't that she looked like MacLaw's dead wife, for she didn't. She didn't look like any girl he could remember ever having seen before. It wasn't even *what* she looked like that made him notice her. It was the way she looked at him. As if she had been completely occupied with her own business and had him well in the back of her mind and then suddenly had seen him and stopped in pleasure to smile at his unexpected appearance before her. And the feeling was on him in brief consciousness that they both knew each other—as plain a feeling as it was ridiculous in fact—for they did not. But it was like that room you come into in a strange house with the certain knowledge that you have been there before and yet you know it cannot be and that the illusion lies in similarity of line or cornice to a room you have known elsewhere.

Whatever it was, it passed between them and they had both felt it momentarily with a mutuality that is embarrassing to strangers. Color flushed the girl's cheekbones.

The doctor looked away as quickly as he had looked at her, for nothing like that happens twice to a man and he was wise enough to know it. He took the troop through town to the flats above the river. "This is your bivouac area, Sergeant Elliott. Twos. Twos right into line. Trumpeter, sound the Halt!" The six note up-and-down ripple tore the afternoon air with a brass knife and the troop halted. "Give me your attention." The Doctor kneed his horse dead center of the line and turned him. "You've been sixteen days on the trail. You've got seven more days to go, before you rejoin the regiment at Fort Starke. Don't tangle with the infantry tonight unless it's forced on you. Don't lose the fight, if it is." He smiled, and the smile faded as quickly.

Bledsoe, the horseholder of the third set of fours, whispered with unmoving lips, "You're the doctor!"

"That's all," MacLaw said. "Sergeant Elliott, take over. I'll make my call on the infantry regimental commander now."

Then Elliott gave it to them, for what he knew was going to happen when he first saw the convoy. "Go ahead," he said, "get on down there as fast as you can after guard mount. Get your bellies full of scoot-a-wa-boo till it runs out your ears. Next, start messin' around with the married women. If there ain't enough to go 'round, start roping the fillies. Get your heads cracked open, your teeth knocked out, get the Rappahannock runs and the Memphis measles and lay yourselves open to every charge in the book, when I get you to Starke. But you'll get to Starke, don't fear, starting like the captain said, one half hour after reveille, ridin' high, far and handsome, drunk or sober, conscious or unconscious, stewed, brewed or tattoed." First Sergeant Elliott drew a long breath and wiped the troop with his eyes, right to left and back to right again. Then he said "Dismiss."

Going back through the town to the ford across the river, Robert MacLaw felt a slight depression thread through him. Not for the future, but for the past. He had a consciousness of living beyond his time, of too many men having passed in his footsteps, leaving him to go on alone, without them. Thirty-seven years old only, but he'd fought Stuart in those years and seen blood drenching the Peninsula and Northern Virginia. He'd been at the Owen Thursday Massacre and he'd been in Mexico on the Massarene Raid. Cohill, Pennell, Topliff, Allshard, Sitterding and Brittles—those were the old regimental names. All gone now, somewhere else, with new faces replacing them and himself the only live ghost to haunt their memories.

He knew it was part sundown, part empty stomach and part the monotonous days on the trail from Fort Pinney, but mostly it was this infantry regiment which was here at Cashman's, for the same reason that he had packed his hospital panniers and left his practice at Mesa and La Paz to put on the blue coat again and rejoin, when his orders arrived after the Custer Massacre. It was all to do over again, and too many wars aren't good for a man's soul.

But that wasn't what he was thinking about at all. That was what he put into his mind to cover the bright smile of that tall girl, for you cannot have a young woman's face pop out at you from between two wagons, and let the memory of it linger. Besides, she did not in the least, look like gentle Molly, except for the smile, perhaps, and the straight carriage of the shoulders and the quick flick of hand to brush back her hair. She was stronger than Molly, more vital, with a greater intensity of womanhood, and MacLaw, from his years of civil practise, knew that for the pure gold it was, for there is a desperation that haunts women and a defeat that lurks just beyond their hopes in youth. That is why most of them are made for the long haul, to carry them on in spite of it. They can only bargain once, and win, lose or draw, they put all they have on the table.

His real trouble was that, like the troopers, he wanted time now and there was no time. He did not want to have seen her here in Cashman's, poised as they all were for to-morrow's move out. He wanted desperately to have met her in La Paz or Mesa where there were the elements of permanence and the ingredients for living life. And it startled him, for that impulse was long behind him and he had gone on from its tragedy in carefully schooled loneness of living, making each day work for itself with none of that integration with yesterday, or to-morrow which builds the chimera of permanency for the family man.

The regimental adjutant was a pink-cheeked lad fresh from the Hudson River Valley with the precision of his schooling stubbornly untarnished. Name of O'Hirons, and MacLaw was glad he hadn't seen Forsythe die, for how could it benefit a youngster to know the long and dusty road that lies ahead? Mr. O'Hirons took MacLaw to the regimental commander's tent.

"MacLaw, sir," the doctor said. "Commanding D Troop. We're on the road from Fort Pinney under orders to rejoin the Regiment at Fort Starke. I'm bivouacking tonight outside of Cashman's, across the river. We move out southward again at five A.M."

Now, the infantry is its own proud breed and Colonel Janeway was an old dog of that breed. He stepped from the door of his tent and took a pace or two, the better to look MacLaw over, and MacLaw was brutally glad that he was properly dressed under his trail filth.

"You're not under arms, sir!"

"No, sir," MacLaw said. "My troop is in bivouac. This is a personal call, sir. On you, as the senior officer present in the vicinity."

The quick blood of anger flushed the colonel's cheeks at his own mistake. He controlled it, but MacLaw didn't like the symptom, for the colonel was too old a man to hold firmly to blood that flooded him that fast.

The colonel said, "You keep your yellow legs on your side of the ford! I'll keep my people this side of it. Besides" —he laughed— "I want dry feet in the morning. I'm moving out for the Paradise River at five A.M." He growled all but the laugh, and it was as if the colonel was offering that laugh in apology for his quick temper. That, the doctor didn't like either, for he knew suddenly that with age, the colonel had become two men, one that betrayed him and the other that was impelled to excuse the betrayal. With an aging body, the colonel fought back eternally for the fragment of youth left in his mind in faint echo. And when he could not find the full shout, he apologized for the search. But the conflict within him kept him at sword's point with himself, causing the stiffness of his muscles, and reviling the futile desire to have them limber again. He was like a man committed to beard dye who hates his dishonesty, for the lie he has committed himself to, but is helpless to face the ridicule of exposure. Too many wars again, MacLaw thought, with the ghosts of Captain Janeway at Cerro Gordo and of Major Janeway of the Peninsula and Gettysburg gibbering eternally at Colonel Janeway at Cashman's from the gathering shadows of sixty odd years, while the man within cowered in the ultimate fear of giving up, of letting go, of crawling back home to a fireside, a stick, a bed, and of passing the dream on to younger men who could still believe in it.

"And," the colonel said, "Department, on top of it all, has had the audacity to order me to take that blasted emigrant convoy with me!" Clean-shaven except for two great horns of mustache, eternally bowed by his tugging hands, the colonel stood there, his blouse buttoned tightly over his slightly balled stomach, as if he was waiting for the doctor to deny it.

Pleasantly enough, the doctor said, "That will be a good sixteen days' march to the Paradise, sir."

And that, apparently, was all the sympathy the colonel needed to unload the rest of his troubles. It was as if he had been waiting there for a stranger to come by, just for that purpose. Someone not of his regiment, that he might confide in. "Four days off the train at Ferguson, from St. Louis!" the colonel growled. "My senior battalion commander down with an infected foot, and sent back! Four officers in the whole regiment who've ever been west of the Mississippi before! Recruit firing incomplete! Enough ammunition in my wagons to blow Texas off the map—and twenty per cent of it rotten, at a guess—stored in warehouses since Appomattox! And now, a civilian wagon convoy and herd to take with me!"

His face was black again with anger. He stared fiercely at the doctor, and the doctor was extremely glad that he was going to have no part of this clambake himself.

There was an infantry runner jogging down toward the ford on the Cashman's side of the river. He splashed across ankle deep, throwing glistening red sheets of water in the blazing sunset.

There was nothing for the doctor to say, so he said nothing, and because he did, the colonel fixed him with a beady eye. "And what bad news do you bring me from Fort Pinney?"

"Nothing from Pinney, sir, but"—he turned and pointed —"I brought D Troop over Boot Notch two hours ago, and on top of the ridge we spotted Indian smoke eleven miles north and east. 'Enemy in the country,' the smoke said, sir."

"So? Who's the enemy? You or me?"

"It has to be your regiment, sir. Two days ago we had a stiff brush with an Arapahoe hunting party. So they knew about us, two days ago."

"God damn it!" the colonel said. "And still it comes! Captain, I envy you your trip south. Will you have a drink?"

He opened the top of his camp box and brought out a gallon jug of Old Mogollon. He put two heavy glasses on the table top and set the jug beside them and laced his fingers across his stomach for that brief pause of anticipation of a man who holds his drinks strictly to just enough and strictly to after Retreat. And with his tongue tip wetting the corners of his lips, he said, "Cavalry I've never understood. How a man can want to go to war encumbered with a stupid horse, is more than I can sabe. Horse just hasn't got sense. Only emotion. If he likes you, he's like a damned woman. Follows you around in a daze. If he doesn't like you—just like a damn woman—beat hell out of him 'till you break his spirit and he still doesn't like you, just broken, that's all. Hell. Spent six years goin' to school in Kentucky on a horse with my four brothers behind me. Never been on one since. Never will. Had enough trouble campaignin' on my two feet, without a horse in one hand and a bag of oats in the other!"

Below them, the runner saluted Lieutenant O'Hirons and the adjutant came sprinting towards them, papers in hand. "What is it now, Mr. O'Hirons?"

"Department, sir, with a telegraphic confirmation from Fort Starke." The colonel snatched at the papers and squint-eyed quickly through them. Then he stared at MacLaw. "You'd better, captain!"

"Better what, sir?" MacLaw asked him.

"Better have that drink. I asked Department for a troop of cavalry to screen my march north, when they wrapped that emigrant convoy around my neck. They have given it to me. Your regiment pulled out of Fort Pinney to where I'm going. Your troop, sir, is ordered to be the screening troop. Pour deep, captain!" and a smile lashed the Old Man's face.

MacLaw almost said *"Doctor,* not captain," but he checked himself from a lifetime of habit. Never frighten a patient unduly if you can help it. For he was not sure that Colonel Janeway's arteries could take any further load. He realized suddenly that he was *not* properly dressed. At Fort Pinney, the only shell jacket he could get in the time he had was a line officer's jacket.

The colonel filled MacLaw's glass and caught his camp stool with his foot, kicking it to hand and motioning his guest to sit. He lowered himself gratefully to his cot and raised his own glass. MacLaw drank and he knew suddenly that the colonel was gloating deep inside at the suddenness of the order that committed someone else to the same stew-pot he was broiling in. It pleased Janeway mightily that the long arm of authority had reached out and snared this detached troop of cavalry and altered its immediate destiny.

The knowledge put the Doctor on the defensive, and the drink rimmed it with quick caution. By his own admission the colonel was running a one man show. By regulations, the troop now became part of the act, under the colonel's thumb. If he admitted that he was a medical officer and not a line officer, it left one choice only to the colonel, to place one of his own infantry officers in command of the troop. Dead men's confidence aside, the thought was unspeakable to MacLaw after the years he had served with the regiment and the past days he had ridden and fought with the troop. Doctor or not, at least his accustomed thinking was cavalry thinking, and with a long trek like this into cavalry country it was out of the question to turn the men over to a dough-foot. Out of the question, that is, with the first welcome bite of the drink.

Colonel Janeway whipped around suddenly, bottle in hand, a tiny dollop squirting from the neck of it, as if he had read the doctor's mind. "And none of your cavalry glory hunting!" the colonel said. "I've got an order to join General Cook as speedily as possible. That means march, not *fight*. Don't you make the mistake of getting me involved in a fight. Do you know how a cavalry screen operates with infantry? Can you command one properly, with your eyes on the main mission of getting me through? *Can you?*"

There was a slight thread of anger in the doctor's own mind, for he was suddenly conscious that the clean and ordered and well-aligned camp that lay about them was the colonel's answer to his own doubts of himself. He had brought the garrison habit with him and set it down boldly at Cashman's as a defense against what lay ahead of him. The doctor knew—and he knew the colonel knew—that tomorrow would see this command on the road in dust and sweat and field bivouacs, and that what worth there was underneath it would erode free of spit and polish, to stand naked and to function without its trimmings. And he knew that he was angry at himself for not saying, "*Doctor*, not captain," and getting out of it, because he was tempted now to defend his position fully, tempted to say, "I have served with my regiment for many years; most of it in the field out here on active service."

He was tempted to point out to the colonel that ever since Appomattox, practically the entire appropriation for the Army had been poured into the cavalry funnel, until at one time almost the entire United States Army had been cavalry and for the best of reasons. Its function on the frontier of the plains country was to contain, control and eventually destroy the finest light cavalry the world had ever seen since the time of Ghengis Khan, the Plains Indians. For he knew those Indians for the men they were in the field, not the reviled savages the eastern newspapers pictured them to be, as they called contemptuously for their extermination. He knew them to have definite controlled tactics and a ruthlessness of purpose that transcended all formalities of war. Past masters of the ruse, the surprise attack and the ambush, for one reason alone, the necessity to win piecemeal or lose the crumbling last vestige of their birthright. He was tempted to say, "I am aware of the sanctity of an order, and of the sacredness of men's lives, sir." And that made him angry at his own anger, for the picture was before him again of Royal Forsythe dying by the trailside, in full trust of him when he gave him Troop D to take in.

So what Doctor MacLaw actually said was, "I should like to ask you a question, sir, before I answer yours, if I may? Have you a cavalry officer in your command that you would prefer to give the screen to?" and he waited for his hide to be chewed out.

Colonel Janeway roared, "I haven't even got an officer who can sit a standing horse! Except my adjutant—and I wouldn't trust him to command a squad until I beat the schoolboy out of him!" He poured the drinks again. "And let me tell you something more. I expect the *worst* from you. I have been forty-two years in the Army, sir—and I have made it a practice always to expect the worst. Only *twice* have I been disappointed!"

The doctor smiled. "Three," he said, "was a sacred number among the ancients. To the north bank of the Paradise, sir!" and he drank, and set his glass down on the field table as he rose to his feet. "Thank you, sir," and he picked up his hat.

He went slowly back through the infantry camp, crossed the ford in the last of the light and came up past the emigrant bivouac that grew through and around the little settlement like vines in shaded foliage, climbing through it for a better place of life in a better sun. The thought of the girl was full upon him now, for she would be there in the march column as he would, and he knew they would meet in the days to come. Suddenly he didn't want that to be, for he had never opened his life but once, and he had no volition to open it ever again. The door was closed too tightly. There was no ability left in him to prise it open—and even if there were, there would be nothing inside. And at first glance, he knew that no casualness would be possible with her. It is that way with some women and it would be with her. For there was more worth taking than you could throw aside. It is never the hurt you do the woman by passing on; it is the hurt you do to yourself. For the woman's hurt is quick and unbelievable and torn full wide in the awful crush of emotion, but a man's hurting haunts him down the years and he never comes quite free of it in his soul.

CHAPTER THREE

D Troop escorted Lieutenant Forsythe to the town cemetery with due honors. Slow march, with boots turned to the rear on his led horse, and Doctor MacLaw recited the Twenty-Third Psalm—all that remained to him of his boyhood religion. But because they had to use ball ammunition, only one man fired the three shots—Gottschalk, the longest service man in the Troop— three times regimental sergeant major, three times busted—and the trumpeter only flatted once on to Extinguish Lights—that regiment didn't use the newfangled Taps.

There wasn't much of an estate. A few weapons. A little money. And among the few dogeared books there was a sort of scrapbook marked Notes. Doctor MacLaw wrote his letter: "First Lieutenant Forsythe died gallantly in line of duty as an officer and a gentleman," and so on, and left the packet with the telegrapher to be forwarded by stage to the post adjutant at Fort Starke. But he kept the book marked Notes, for it held a rather amazing collection of military memorabilia. Clippings, whole pages out from Philip St. George Cooke's Cavalry Tactics, and quoted comments of the Prince Kraft zu Hohenlohe—Igelfingen such as: "The object of the cavalry screen is to keep all hostile parties from penetrating, and by moving forward to gain contact with the enemy and keep it. The line of squads must be continuous and held close to the supports."

And for the first time in his life, Doctor MacLaw felt a deep and scientific respect for the line officer. Here was no megalomaniac, with drawn sabre and shouting voice, but rather a careful fellow who made meticulous notes of his operations, referred in his own work to authoritative source and proceeded to the job at hand with a technician's studied precision.

But it was, in a way, a specialist's reference work, not a country doctor's *vade mecum*, for its printed excerpts carried a rather academic flavor. If such and such a move were made against you, you made such and such a counter move, as if warfare were a game of chess played to tournament rules. Apparently Lieutenant Forsythe had taken some exception to this flavor himself, for at the foot of a printed academic discussion of the functions of cavalry he had written: "Hogwash! *Find* 'em. *Fend* 'em. *Fix* 'em and *finally finish* 'em—or words to that effect! R. G. Forsythe."

The doctor smiled, for it had been apparent to him that what Forsythe had objected to was what he had objected to in his own profession since his student days—the screening of cause and effect, method and accomplishment by the fringe of insanity of words. Somewhere, if you searched for it avidly, you always found the common sense approach which paid off in results. But invariably there is a tendency in man to shroud his own fraternity of endeavor in the esoteric jargon of specialized words, obscure to the uninitiated.

It was under the lamp in the telegraph office that he thumbed through the notebook and decided to keep it. There was still some after-light when he stepped outside. There was a sobbing woman in his path, head bent, with two other women supporting her, walking with her, and several other women in a trailing group behind. All of them with rather sad little clutches of prairie flowers in hand. Drab women, worn with families and work. Grim-lipped and gnarled of hand. But on a solemn mission and calling attention to it solemnly, in the way women call attention to their militant piety when they go to church.

MacLaw stepped back to the edge of the short run of duckboard, and his right boot came down heavily through rotted wood, snapping it off at the other side so that the board flashed up like the blade of a jacknife. There was a soft scream of surprise more than pain as he teetered for a moment, flailing his arms for balance, and ridiculously he saw the tall wagon girl trying desperately to regain her own balance on the opposite side of the walk, saw her crouch in a half desperate twist of her body and sit to keep herself from plunging headlong into the rutted street. Then he was stooped over her, and she was looking up at him with controlled and silent laughter in her eyes.

"Now say it," she said.

"Are you hurt?" he asked her. "Say what?"

"Just that," she smiled. "Everyone always does. 'Are you hurt?' "

He laughed. "Well, *are* you?"

"In my dignity only. What exactly happened?"

"A stupid thing," he said. "I stepped in the wrong place apparently, and a board thrust up and struck you."

She shook her head. "Not that easy. My foot went through an empty space, and I'm caught in it like a muskrat. What do you suppose I do about it?"

"If I lift you, perhaps you can get free." The small procession of weeping women had passed on and they were alone. He stepped behind her and put his hands firmly under her arms, his head bent to hers, the fresh starch of her bonnet and the warm wheaten scent of her hair in his nostrils. She smelled clean and young and warmly female and the hunger was on him like a shout in silence, flooding him full like the pain of the knife. For a moment he stooped there, his hands on her, and then he heard his voice harsh in his held breath, "Ready?"

"I think so."

He lifted her heavily, for the sudden frenzy in his own taut muscles, pulled her upright against him. She turned half sideways, twisting the trapped foot, getting it lengthwise between the boards, freeing it, and for another second they stood there. Then the laughter went out of her eyes, like a blown candle in the ancient defense of women, and she said, "Thank you. I'm afraid I was heavy," and faint color touched her cheekbones.

He dropped his hands, and there was the sudden screaming revolt inside him that this game must always be played and that man himself had made the rules. His laughter cackled in the darkness.

"It is ridiculous, isn't it?" she said. To get one's foot caught?"

"It is," he nodded solemnly. "Are these your flowers?" He bent down and began to gather the wispy prairie blooms. She stood above him as he picked them up one by one, and as she watched his easy movements she knew that she had searched for him with her eyes, half shamefully, ever since she had first seen him when the cavalry soldiers rode into Cashman's, yet with no real shame, for the impulse was deep in her to laugh at the shallow, theatrical modesty of women. But somehow now, there was real shame, and she loathed the thought that he had seen it in her. Loathed the knowing that she must cover it with cold formality.

He had the flowers now and he held them out to her, and she saw faint mockery in his eyes and knew that it was there because he knew her thinking. It was as if he stood there deliberately waiting for her to put it into words. As if he had said, "You can't very well turn and run like a doe, can you? Of course you can't, for you are a civilized young woman and civilized young women can't do that. But that's what you want to do—run from me. You won't though. Instead you will change the subject, become immediately impersonal about the whole incident. Impress upon me that you are a well brought up young lady and that that fact at once precludes all possibility of humanity."

So she put it into words. Cold. Serious. She said, "Do excuse my boldness, sir, but this evening—wasn't there a service for a dead soldier?"

"There was, ma'am," Robert MacLaw bowed.

"Would it be fitting," she held up the pitiful flowers, "if we left a few—for him?"

"But indeed yes," he said. "It would be a kindly gesture—for a woman." Then he nodded to the women who had gone on and there was a question in his eyes.

"A little boy," the girl said. "He died this morning. We move early tomorrow into the Paradise country with Colonel Janeway's regiment. It is the last time his mother may go to his grave."

Death in children did something to the doctor that he had never quite got over. It always made him try to find reason why a life should end before it had started the full journey.

"Of what," he asked gently, "did the little boy die?"

The girl said, "He died quite suddenly before we really knew he was very ill."

"He just died—without being sick?"

"No," she said. "He was ailing a day or so. He had fever and chills and he was sick to his stomach."

Rather quickly the doctor asked, "Was there by any chance a backache or a rash? Are others ill in your party? Have you a doctor among you?"

She closed her eyes tightly for a second. "My father was a doctor," she said. "He died just before we left Missouri. There is a grown man ill of chills and fever. The regimental surgeon says grippe. Is there smallpox about?"

"Good Lord, I don't think so," the doctor smiled. "But I was caught in it once, and once caught, always wary."

"I too," she said. "It leaves one frightened. The little boy died so quickly. I saw no rash. He did not complain of backache. For many illnesses," she held her head high, "my father taught me the rudiments. I suppose I could call myself a nurse."

The doctor smiled. "If you are a good nurse," he said, "you will put absolute trust in your doctor, the regimental surgeon, and you will not worry. I shall take you on up to the cemetery, to your friends."

"There is no need," she said primly.

"On the contrary," he said. "There is every need. You are much too pretty a girl to walk alone through a bivouac of dog-faced soldiers." And the mocking smile. "For you might meet another one."

"You are bold yourself, sir."

"Yes," he said, "and therefore I shall take you on up the street." Then she turned from him to hide her flaming cheeks, and head high in anger, walked on with MacLaw beside her in the darkness. "My name," he said, "is Robert MacLaw. I think you should know that, for I am going to the Paradise country, too, and we cannot avoid meeting again."

After a moment, she said, "Martha Cutting."

"I find that a good sounding name," he told her. "There is a gentleness and a harshness to it, in even blend—as if at once to invite and warn. *My* name has always sounded to me like four cuts of a broad axe—*Rob-ert Mac-Law*—to warn only."

"Against what?" she asked him.

"Against a forbidding dourness that lives too much in intro-spection, and that would never in the world have allowed me to walk with you as I am now, if I didn't know fully that you wanted me to."

Martha stopped suddenly and turned full toward him. It was quite dark now, and they were beyond the settlement lights. Just ahead was the cemetery, with the other women grouped in a light of flickering candles they shielded with their hands. She wanted to say "I did want you to." But instead she said, "There are my friends now. Thank you."

He took off his battered hat and held it easily against his thigh. She could see the faint pinpoints of the candles reflected in his eyes. There was no mockery in them now. For a moment neither of them spoke, and, as the moment lengthened, there was no embarrassment as there would have been with strangers. It was as if he waited merely. And the impulse was frighteningly strong for her to put out her hand and lay it upon his arm, knowing that he would cover it in gentle kindliness.

"You asked me," he said, "if it would be fitting to leave flowers for a soldier. Let me tell you that the dead are alive again in this world, only when the hands and the minds of the living choose to remember them in kindness. The dead soldier's name was Raymond Forsythe, lieutenant of cavalry, if it is in your mind to leave a prayer as well as flowers. He had no family. Good night, Martha."

Reveille on the C Trumpet tore the thin frost off the bivouac of the troop at three-thirty the next morning, and before its echo died, a big infantry G bugle answered it full-throatedly across the river.

On the beginning of the echo, the men were out of it, stumbling blind in the darkness of the troop's area, hawking and cursing scarlet, but falling in steadily, along the line of saddles for First Sergeant Elliott's roll call, with the automatic precision of regulars. They stood dank in the armpits, with sour alcohol staining the air, and vomit close down their throats, but they stood steady, come back to the template of discipline that held them and concealed the scoot-a-wa-boo they had drunk and the half-breed Pawnee doxie they had found, whose sweat stench was dried on twenty-six of them in a row at two-bits a gallop with the two-headed beast.

They were blear-eyed and bruised, mat-burned and knuckle-cut, with the white worms crawling in their steaming gut, but they got their place in the line and snapped it out when the United States called their name, for that was all they had left now. There was still an outside, but it was too big for them, too loose, and they couldn't get a purchase. So they came into the runway, where they fit tight, and they made their contract to stand steady for the duty, slug and run wild again when the gate opened at the next stop. "D Troop all present or accounted for!"

There were lantern lights all over Cashman's and the growl of great wagon wheels in the streets and a disorder of people. While D Troop fed and broke camp to stand to horse, MacLaw looked at the men's gray morning faces—the unsung faces of empire. Runaway wife beaters and thieves and failures in the counting-houses. Cads and castaways and curdle-heads. Thirteen dollars a month for the blue shirt on their backs and no 'Thank you kindly' for any job they did. Bledsoe, Foy, Halliday, MacKenzie, Storrs. What's a name?

"Twos. Twos right. At the walk." Dr. MacLaw took them down past the emigrant wagons, now drawn up in march line, with the oxen hooked in and the outriders mounted around the lowing cattle herd. Took them across the ankle-deep ford to the opposite bank.

Colonel Janeway stood midway of his forming column, sallow-faced with the early hour, pacing the stiffness out of his leg muscles and watching his command with a sour eye. Then it was that you could see the trouble that haunted the old man, for half broken, with some tents down and rolled, some flat and some still standing, the infantry camp looked like a gypsy wagon circle. With time, the recruits had been whipped into some sem-blance of contained order in the camp, but midway the move-out the lack of training was as crippling as a crushed foot. The non-coms lashed in among the men, driving and shouting them into a routine that takes months to wear the raggedness off—and only worsens if you try to hurry it.

There was no time schedule, or if there had been one, it was broken down hopelessly. One company was still on the chow line. Two were formed ready to march, under arms and in full field pack. There was a rabble still milling about the latrines, and a fatigue party loading wagons and yelling for its breakfast. There were fires left smouldering, and there was loose equipment all over the place. But the worst of it was that the only present solution Janeway saw was to keep a finger in all of it himself, and a regimental commander who chooses to be a first sergeant is a lost ball in the tall weeds at the start; for no man can do it nor last long even trying to.

"Major Irish! Tell that man it's not a pole axe he's carrying; it's a rifle!"

Doctor MacLaw rode in and dismounted. "MacLaw, sir. With the screen. Have you any special orders?"

The colonel looked him over again and, this time he saw a holstered hand gun on the doctor's duty belt. "Have you everything you need, captain? Rations? Forage? Ammunition?"

"For seven days we shall be all right on rations and forage, sir. And we have five hundred rounds of ammunition per carbine in our escort wagons. All there was at Fort Pinney."

"Put your escort wagons in my regimental train. Tell Mr. O'Hirons when you need forage and rations. This is my order of march. First and second battalions leading, with an advance guard company a thousand yards ahead. Then the regimental wagon train. After that the civilian convoy and cattle herds. The third battalion, Major Ingraham, marches at the rear, less one company, Captain McCluskey. That company marches in file on either side of the emigrants to keep them from straggling. I want you to fan your troop out ahead of the advance guard and along the right flank of my line of march as far as it will go. Roughly three thousand yards out. I estimate my rate of march at three and a half miles an hour today. Four miles tomorrow. I intend to keep it on its feet twelve full hours each day, exclusive of halts. Half-hour halt for cold noon mess. Housekeeping halts ten minutes in each hour."

It had the memorized formality of a written order as the colonel droned it off, as if that was the way he had said it would be and that was the way they would do it, or else. It denied all elements of humanity or chance and stood forth stolidly like garrison routine, with the guard house directly behind it to enforce it. But suddenly the old forgotten field soldier that had been the colonel in youth, stalked around the corner of it.

"Keep your eye on the Estrella foothills, captain, where that Indian smoke was last night. My column will be five and a half miles long. My first and second Battalions are separated from the third by three miles of noncombatant convoy. That's the better part of an hour's separation, in infantry time. Bear that in mind in case of trouble. And bear it in mind that I don't want trouble, because trouble means deployment of elements of the column and deployment means loss of march time. I intend to report myself to General Cook by the 20th instant. Are there any questions?"

"No, sir. Thank you, sir." MacLaw mounted and kneed around to his waiting troop and skirted it off to the northward in close order. But from the book in the doctor's pocket an insistent phrase shadowed across his brain: "As a general rule, infantry has no mobility with which to choose suitable fighting terrain, except the mobility inherent in its marching potential, which must always be carefully planned in advance and can seldom be replanned after action is joined. In other words, the foot soldier must fight where he stands."

Academic or not, the doctor thought, *that's exactly what the colonel was trying to tell me.* But it was only a shadow in his mind, for what was really worrying him was that he ought to see that sick man in the convoy that Martha Cutting had told him about, for the antismallpox phial in the doctor's pannier wasn't enough to scratch one company. That worried him, for he had awakened thinking of the dead child they were leaving behind with Forsythe in the settlement cemetery, and trying again to search his mind for justification of death in children. He found none—but found again the eternal challenge of the physician to establish cause and thereby thwart further effect. But he wasn't a physician any longer, nor would he be again until the emergency was over and the blue coat hung again on its closet hook. For in the Army, there are only surgeons.

The dawn came up with its vast and silent explosion behind D Troop as it rode stolidly at the walk behind him, and the mists ahead lifted from the face of the west and left it naked in all its stark and frightening beauty. Antelope jacks raced off on both flanks of the march, and the ground underfoot commenced to dry slowly from its thin film of night dew to powder presently into gray dust that muddied up the mounts' legs where the long grass had wet them. Instinctively, the doctor raised his eyes to the Estrellas for Indian smoke, but there was none.

"Sergeant Elliott." The doctor halted and swept his arm forward and down to the right of the vast prairie ahead, holding it straight out from his side toward the Estrellas. "I shall want D Troop spread from dead ahead on the march line to as far down on the right flank of the march as I am pointing to. What I would like is to have the men in squad formation of some sort, with the line of squads continuous and held in close to the support squads. But I realize that is impossible with only forty-seven men."

The sergeant nodded with a slightly querulous look in his eye. "That's what it says in the book, sir."

The doctor looked closely at Elliott, but there was no mockery in the man.

"Put it this way, sergeant. I want a formation across the front and right that will allow no hostile scout parties to get between us and the column."

"Well, sir, the only sure thing then is a line of skirmishers extended to hand-signal distance. And hold one squad out with us, for support, in case we're penetrated."

"Give the appropriate order then, Sergeant Elliott. And one thing more. I want a small scout group of our own, to move well out ahead of us toward the hills. I believe the phrase is 'make contact with the enemy and keep it.' "

"That's in the book, too, sir."

"What book, sergeant?"

The sergeant grinned. "The book, sir that you throw away when they issue you ball ammunition. Does the captain have any further orders, sir?"

"That will be it, sergeant; the skirmishers will walk their horses all day at no faster than three and a half miles an hour, and every man in the troop will at all times be able to see the man to his right and to his left."

And there it was as the sun came up behind. Six hundred doughfoots slogging in a long clot of gray dust, seventy-four civilian men, women and children breathing it, one hundred and four wagons, and a herd of beef cattle. With forty-seven cavalry-men out on a limb ahead and beside it, with the whole West to Wyoming to move into.

CHAPTER FOUR

CORPORAL Fleming took the advance scout party—Dannecker, Nikirk, Storrs and Gottschalk—and keeping the new sun as well to their backs as possible, they rode out of it toward the Estrellas, using draws and rises to mask their right shoulders. Fleming was an odd numbered man who had always known exactly what he wanted out of life. Seven years with the troop and he had the two stripes he wanted. Seven years more and he'd make sergeant. Twenty years even and he'd be top soldier to rule the world he lived in for the final twenty-two years of his service. Then at sixty, he'd go back to Marblehead, on his retired pay, and spit full in the face of the town that had tried to make a sailor out of him and had spit in *his* face because he told them flat that only fools froze and baked in season with the fish boats, or took the long runs for a hell on earth at sea and lost their work-pay in the first port they lifted.

There was no tar on Fleming's hands and there never would be on his soul. So let the old men sit around and lie the same lies and talk eternally, so that their talk washed monotonously and unheard half the time, like the Atlantic when you lived by it. But when his time came to talk, they'd damn well listen for he'd have a tale to spin that was in none of their lives. And when they said, "How come you settled in Marblehead, Sarge?" he'd spit and tell 'em, "Hell, I was born here, but I was wise enough to git out, before I got drowned."

By nine o'clock, Fleming was dismounted and lying close on the lip of a draw, the horses below and Gottschalk beside him, watching the western end of the Pass of the Maidens. There was thick dust high inside the pass when they first got into position, but it was only a matter of minutes before they saw what caused the dust. Gottschalk held his hat toward the sun to throw shadow on the lenses of Fleming's glasses, so there would be no glint and he said, "Saint Christopher and Cump Sherman! That's a lot of hostiles!"

"A lot ain't good enough, Gottschalk. I gotta git *how* many. You heard the doctor." So they lay there and watched and the sun rose high and hot and the sweat from their armpits dissolved the white salt rime on their frayed shirts and they could smell each other—like wet saddles in a sour pickle vat—and Fleming said, "That movement's two miles long, and it ain't cleared the pass yet. You stink, Gotts-chalk. Put a flower behind your ear."

Old Gottschalk turned and looked at the corporal. It had been twenty years since he had worn his own first pair of stripes—and lost them as easily as he had got them. He'd gone all the way up to sergeant major and down again three times, until it was an old story in his mind. There wasn't anything about the trade he didn't know; there wasn't a short cut in any of it that he hadn't found out about long ago, knowing fully the ones that worked and the ones that invariably trapped a man. Best of all, he knew how to keep alive and how to stay content and neither came from wearing stripes.

Take your thirteen dollars a month as a trooper and let somebody else stay behind as a dead hero for the responsibility he wore on his arm. Let somebody else stay up nights figuring out shortages brought about by a malingerer under your command.

"Fleming," he said, "you try too hard. You work at it like a job. You don't want to do that, boy, because it ain't a job; it's a habit of mind, like. It takes time and experience and luck to get the habit." He spat. "You can't tell when you got it yourself, but you can sure as hell tell it in another man!"

"How, fer Cris' sake?"

"When he stinks like me," Gottschalk chuckled and he put his glasses on the hostile column again. "Araphoes and Cheyennes, with the outriders stripped to gee strings, ready to fight—and you know what? Something no recruit never seen this far before—Pawnees!"

"Don't get superior, pop." Fleming flicked his chevrons with the fingers of his left hand.

"I'm telling you!" Gottschalk said. "They got the tepees folded on the travois poles in the front part of the column, but"—he held his arm out with two fingers spread—"look right of my right finger. They got travois poles dragging, but no big lumps of folded tepee skins on 'em. Parfleches only. Pawnees live in dirt huts at home, bub, and wattle wickiups on the move. That'll also probably mean Omahas and Sacs and Foxes and mebbe Otos with 'em. They're all cousins way back—like girls in Georgia."

"An old man like you!" the corporal said.

"I got more time in the guardhouse than you got in the Army!"

"Be friendly," Fleming said, "get along with me."

"Sure"—Gottschalk nodded—"I will. I'll tell you something friendly. If you don't drag pratt out of here fast, the paymaster'll scratch your name." And as he spoke, a narrow sickle of brown horsemen flashed out from the Indian mass at the gallop on a wide arc toward them, to cover the tribes' march.

Fleming watched them come toward his observing position with a feeling that it wasn't quite real. It did that to you. Impending action was sort of like this hypnotism you read about; it held you entranced, for a moment or two, so that you had no conscious power to think.

He knew what was coming—knew that shrieking murder rode each pony, with repeating rifles and trade knives of razor steel, and he knew what it was to be caught by what was coming for he'd seen men who'd been caught. Seen 'em try to talk with a tongue cut out. Seen 'em with their eyelids sliced off. But for a moment, it still wasn't quite real, for it was distant still, fraught with swift and awful grandeur until it had a stark beauty of its own.

Then fear spattered over him like somebody else's blood in the heat of action, and he had to tighten himself inside to brace against it. Gottschalk felt him tighten, heard him draw the deep whistling breath into his lungs for steadiness. And Gottschalk winked, "O.K., boy, you're the corporal. Be the hero."

"Shut up!" Fleming shouted at him, and then he called back, "Shake the dung, Nikirk!" and the scout party scrambled to horse and galloped back along the draw toward D Troop's skirmish line.

Corporal Fleming wrote all of it out with a stub pencil soaked in labored spit, and sent Nikirk back in with it. Doctor MacLaw riding dead center of his long, thin line read the estimate and put his own glasses on the distant dust of the Indian march. Estimating forty percent of the mass movement to be squaws and children—Colonel Janeway was paralleling the line of march of twelve hundred of the finest light cavalry in the world, outnumbered by them, two to one. Paralleling it at fourteen miles' distance and about four hours ahead of it, so that any slight deviation of Janeway's march to the west—or of the Indians'—would lay the mass of hostiles across the regiment's rear.

Colonel Janeway rode no horse; he slogged at the head of his regiment. He kept his battalion commanders on foot, too. "You've got feet, use 'em." Young Mr. O'Hirons he let lead a horse, between running errands on top of it. "Mr. O'Hirons," he said, "get on that animal and take this message from the screen back to Major Ingraham in the rear battalion."

O'Hirons galloped down the long column. He loved that. Hat cocked and chin strapped and importance all over him, lancing through the stifling dust clouds, tearing them into trailing skeins that were like the smoke of artillery fire. No one in the first and second battalions even looked at him. How's it go?

"*Aides, acrobats and adjutants*"—but the girls in the emigrant train smiled at him and the mopheaded kids halloed in admiration. He rode on down and gave Major Ingraham the message, pulling his horse up, fore-hooves thrashing, flinging off.

Ingraham was young for his leaf as that Army went, but thirty-four years to the game the hard way. "If you want to be a hero, O"Hirons," he said, "tell the Old Man that Cashman's on fire."

"How's that, sir?"

"Ride back to the rise we just came over and see for yourself. That's how it is. Cashman's is on fire."

Mr. O'Hirons flung himself back on his horse and kneed him back along the line of march to the rise, half a mile behind. He could see the smoke as soon as he topped it, hanging thin in the air like long black hair blown in the wind. Being a book soldier so far, his first thought was that some recruit had left a cook fire, neglecting to put it out, and that it had spread into brush as soon as the wind fanned it up. And it was on him cold that he'd stalk the bivouac as adjutant every morning from now on to be sure all the fires were out. But even as the intent came to him, he knew he was wrong. Cashman's was on fire—set on fire. And he knew why.

For a moment, a dreadful loneliness roared in upon him as he stood on that ridgeline. He could see the dust of the Indian march quite plainly and knew that a war party had dropped back to sack Cashman's as soon as the regiment moved out. He knew it, but he couldn't accept it, for the book was still strong in his mind. It was utterly impossible that these savages dared play ducks and drakes with a regiment in its slow might. Unthinkable.

With doubt still fighting his mind, he galloped back to Major Ingraham.

"How'd you think it caught on fire, sir?"

Major Ingraham initialed the message. "If it was Chicago, I'd say one of those cows kicked over a lantern," and he jerked his head in disgust at the herd that preceded his line of march.

"Yes, sir."

When O'Hirons reported it, the colonel stomped on angrily for twenty cadenced paces in silence, his adjutant leading the horse beside him; then just as if O'Hirons had denied it, he turned and said, "All right, mister; Cashman's is on fire! What do you suggest I do—go back fifteen miles and organize a bucket brigade. I've got a march order!"

Doctor MacLaw saw more than the fire. From his years out in that country, he could see a hostile party watching at dawn from Boot Notch—watching the regiment move out. Letting it get well on its way, before they slipped down through the mists for the work in hand. He could see the wretched fight for what it would have been—hot fire fights from the houses until the guns sucked dry. Arrows, tufted in flaming straw. The screaming circle of horsemen around the tiny town and through it. Heads with torn red mouths on top, and the telegrapher's two girls sobbing in the river bottom, clutching the shreds of clothing left to them, beating their fists in the mud in hopeless agony. For the tribes were up again to pay off the white man's perfidy, and there was still no answer to any of it.

The worst of it with MacLaw was that he had seen too much of it in his lifetime; so when it threatened once again, the pictures of the past were already in his mind to give him focal points to build on. All he had to do was riffle through the file of his experience. He was a sensitive man with imagination, so his experience was vivid. In his own profession, there was cold impersonality, but beyond it, he had the power to suffer acutely in the suffering of others.

The whole business of the frontier was the delicate equation of balance and check. It was wrong that the march of the white man should steal the hunting country of the Indian, but it was wrong, too, that roving bands of nomads should try to hold the entire country in the face of the inexorable westward march of civilization. So at once you had insoluble misbalance, that could only come into temporary equilibrium by compromise. When the scales tipped—check to balance again. But not this time, somehow. And he felt it deeply within him like the presage of death. There was hope once more in the tribes and the visible knowledge of their overwhelming strength. The balance was gone over to them, and they knew it. And so did the doctor.

All through that interminable first afternoon, Doctor MacLaw rode with his thinly spread screen, a sort of quiet fury sitting the pit of his stomach for Cashman's, because there wasn't anything in God's world that he could do about it. The order was: March.

At times, crossing a rise of ground, the doctor could see the high dust of the tribe migration, hanging like the afterblast of a great explosion against the blue foothills of the Estrellas. Twice, long lines of galloping brown horsemen came in close enough for him to see through his glasses, and late in the day, for him to see wet scalps on some of them. He began to get an annoying idea that they were laughing at him, and it stayed with him because they laughed out loud around four o'clock. There was a sharp flurry of repeating-rifle fire out where Corporal Fleming was, punched through with answering carbine fire. Then silence for a count of twenty. Then the whole thing over again, much closer in to the screen.

MacLaw shouted for the support squad to get out after the scout party fast, and he led it out personally, riding for the sound of the firing, leading in at the gallop until he was close enough to scout the position. Corporal Fleming was on a bald knoll, fixed there, with the hostiles beginning to circle widely, ringing him for the kill.

Fleming knew what was coming that time without any sense of unreality about it. He looked chalk-faced at Gotts-chalk. Gottschalk snarled in hideous silent laughter. "Tried to show off once too often, din' ya, boy? Tried to prove them stripes to me, for what ya feel in them? Well, go ahead, prove them!"

"Get down off here and mount up!"

"Sure, sure, which way we go then? The circle's clear around us. To get through, we gotta cut through. And you don't lead us; I'll lead. And you come last to see we get through. That's where ya pay off for the extra dollars ya git each month!"

"Argue with me," Fleming told him, "and I'll shoot out your eyes." He flung up his arm and pointed. "That way, you talkative bastard! There comes the support squad with the captain. Cut toward it. Nikirk, Foy, Dannecker! Mount up and head out!"

Gottschalk riding with Fleming, grinned at him. "Mebbe ya got sense, boy. Just try to grow up with it. That's next!"

The doctor shouted to the trumpeter to sound Recall, and the man drew up sharp and lipped into its metallic finality, hammering it out to Fleming across the distance. Fleming got his party mounted, but he never would have gotten clear, if the doctor hadn't gone all the way in and hauled him out.

You never live it at the time, for there is a curtain that drops and hides the details, and all of it is drawn tight, with a flame-white border around it, so that you can't see beyond, for dry-eyed blindness. But later it comes back, and it is there forever. The screams and the thunder and the gagging hot wind and a shot hitting into a man with the sound of a stick whipped into mud. *"Holy Mary, Mother of God"*—and your own gun firing close into the brown streak beside you, so that you can see the slugs rip into him, but he doesn't let go; he rides like the furies and stinks of sickish spice and of animal hair and of rancid grease, and then thrashes over backward as if he were jerked on a rawhide. And the sweat and the spit laces your cheeks to the ear lobes. And Fleming shouts in your face, but no words. Then you come out of it, cold in shock, but the mounts don't come out of it, for there's blood in their nostrils and they won't let down. "Assemble on me!

Hold it to a trot! Come down, Dannecker! If you can't ride that horse, carry it! Steaday!"

Then you are well out of it and riding free, but it costs. It always costs. It has to cost, and the coin comes high. "Foy, O.M., Trooper—from Duty to Killed in Action"; and no going back, for Corporal Fleming saw him down on one knee, holding his shot-through gut—saw them jump him. But what Fleming won't ever tell, for nobody will ever ask—it was Fleming's shot that smashed Foy's neck, before they cut his hair. "Storrs, E., Trooper—from Duty to Wounded in Action"; and on the Horse Books, Sal written off. "Damn it to hell, Sal always stopped to talk!"

But it was the doctor who knew that they got clear, only because it was petulance and punch and vinegar on the hostiles' part, rather than deep intent. They didn't follow in very far. They kept their distance and kept on laughing.

And the doctor damned well knew why they were laughing. They hadn't seen infantry out there for years, and they had scant respect for it, for only squaws walk. They laughed, for they knew that time marched in their migration and the prospect of loot was magnificent—cattle and the rifles of stragglers, emigrant wagons full of bright gewgaws, ammunition—and women. All they had to do was to laugh and ride out time.

The march column halted at five-thirty, with sore feet and about twenty-seven sullen miles slogged out behind it. Doctor MacLaw sat his horse while the screen drew in and assembled on his position.

He was tired, suddenly, deep in his bones with the infinite fatigue that comes after action, and the men were tired with him. He could feel exhaustion in them like a low keen as they drew up around him, for there can be almost an audible sound to it. Their faces were parboiled over their deep tan with the day's hot sun, and their eyes were red with dust and excitement.

He knew what was worse than the day—it was the knowledge in the troop's minds that the whole set-up was wrong. This was cavalry country, not infantry. But they were tied to the regiment now, with no real function left to them beyond the regiment's function. Slowed to the infantry pace, but with five times the spread of terrain to cover. Condemned to the infantry function, with consequent loss of their own supreme advantage, mobility. And they hated it. Loathed it in their souls.

Alone, they could have evaded the whole tribal march. This way, they had no choice but a repetition of to-day, every day to come, until the march was finished—and with it, the troop finished, too.

Lieutenant O'Hirons rode out. "The colonel's courtesies, sir," he saluted. "He's bivouacking where he is now. Local security to his regiment. He suggests that you withdraw within his line of outguards for the night and feed a hot meal. One half troop at C Company's kitchens, one half at D Company's." MacLaw thanked him. "And the colonel would like to see you personally after Evening Stables." O'Hirons looked wistfully at the horses, for he had missed a choice of cavalry by a scant two files in his class.

Sergeant Elliott put his picket line in on the end of the regimental-wagon-train picket lines. Trooper Storrs they slid out of his bloody saddle, and hopped and walked him to one of their escort wagons. They got his pants down and a belt strap between his teeth, and Doctor MacLaw made his preliminary examination. Storrs had been flat down to his mount's neck at full gallop when he was hit, and with his own tension of muscle, the bullet had torn him like a knife. His buttocks looked like raw beef. MacLaw swabbed with carbolic solution, while Storrs writhed silently under him, two men holding his legs and shoulders. The slug had struck him half way down the right thigh and gone along the bone on an upward course, missing the rectum and missing him vitally and striking through into the left buttock so close to the surface that, flattened by impact, it had torn the flesh open like an axe cut.

MacLaw probed to be sure the bullet was clean out, leaving no soft flakes of lead in its path. Then he sutured and bandaged, and they wrapped Storrs in a blanket, warm against shock, when the whiskey they gave him burned out of him.

"Flat on your face for a week, Storrs, but you're still a whole man." MacLaw grinned at him.

"Man enough," Storrs grunted, "to tell 'em what they can do if they want to pay honor to my wound. Thanks, doc, and I'm damned glad nobody taught the bugger who hit me to allow for windage!"

But that damned horse of Storrs', they couldn't do anything with her. The horse was still for duty, so she kept position in her set of fours and to hell with being led.

Sergeant Elliott booted the troop through Evening Stables. The doctor inspected each mount himself, hooves and backs, and walked up toward the column's head to report himself to Colonel Janeway.

Sergeant Elliott lined up the troop, less the guard detail. "You chow with the beetle crushers," he said. "Mind your lip and your table manners. Two more things: Keep your minds out of those petticoats down in the emigrant convoy. It's off limits for D Troop. I catch a trooper down there, I'll nail his breeks to a stump and kick him over backward. Them women are goin' to get better lookin' every mile west we march, until the ones with the faces that would stop a mule train are goin' to be ravin' beauties. But lay off 'em, you've got work to do and work don't mix with women. You're goin' to see this doughfoot regiment messin' around down there every night with 'em, but that ain't goin' to be an excuse for any of you to cut in on the party.

"The doughfoot regiment ain't fully trained. It's recruits in the main, and it's headed for trouble of all kinds, and if it wants to lose its sleep shackin' up half the night, let it. But not you yellow legs. You keep your vinegar for the saddle, not the sack." He drew in a sharp breath. "We lost a man to-day. That don't come easy to me. Nothin' brings 'em back alive once they stop drawin' pay. Keep your mind fixed on Foy lyin' out there cold and get it firm in your minds we ain't got men to lose! Play this close to the vest. That goes double for the corporals. Play it cozy and play it safe. Fend 'em, but don't try to fix 'em and finally finish 'em—for we can't do it. We ain't got the strength. You're on nursemaid duty, protectin' a convoy. Be nursemaids and don't try to run it out for record. The second thing I've got to say: *Captain* MacLaw commands this troop—not *Doctor*—or I'll nail the rest of you. Because I ain't havin' the infantry sneering at us!"

Colonel Janeway sat on a folded ground sheet, eating out of a meat can. He resented his sixty years bitterly and punished himself continually for them. One blanket. One extra pair of sox. One straight line of thought. He took a Stylites' public pride in forcing upon himself all of the rigors of the march that his men were forced to accept. The only luxury he allowed himself was to let Lieutenant O'Hirons fill the meat can and wash it afterwards.

"MacLaw," he said, "what was that shooting around four o'clock?"

"My scout party got ringed, sir. They forced out too far. We got them back."

The Colonel frowned. "I have an order to join General Cook! Those hostiles aren't going to take a chance fooling around with this regiment, sir—and I'm not going out of my way to stir them up!" His face was livid. "You'd better understand that now, if you didn't when I gave it to you last night! You leave them alone, unless they get after us. Do you hear me? *Do* you!" His voice broke into sharp anger, and he thrust himself up as if he would pound his order into MacLaw with his fists. But he couldn't get up. His whole muscular system was out of control under the furious rush of blood, and he sat there helpless in his rage. Not this time, MacLaw was thinking, but some time that blood will let go and throw him into a mumbling coma, tear his eyelid and his cheek down on one side and leave an arm and a leg. as limp as wet shirts.

"Yes, sir," MacLaw said, and then the colonel was up on his feet and the flood of his betrayal receded, leaving a shadow of shame deep in his eyes.

He said in half apology, "They wasted no time in sacking Cashman's, did they?" He walked around MacLaw in a short half circle, his thumbs plunged into his belt, his heels thrusting deep into the loose soil. "They must have all been in camp below the high point that Indian smoke rose from that you reported to me. Not fifteen miles from me, like hill cats, keeping the sight and the sound of themselves from me, but scouting me out for my move-out, so they could swoop down on the settlement as soon as I left! God damn them for the shifty, shadowy beggars they are. I've fought 'em before, but I'd forgotten, I guess.

"This isn't civilized warfare out here, where you can plan a move against another man's plan and put the outcome on the better military brain. No Indian force in the world would have had a chance at Contreras or Chapultepec against Winfield Scott's brain, for the Mexicans didn't have a chance against the final outcome, did they?" He thrust up his chin at MacLaw. "No, sir! Nor would they have had a chance against Phil Sheridan or 'Cump' Sherman or the Old Man himself. And here I am caught dead to rights with a march order. I couldn't go back to Cashman's, and even if I had, they would have been gone by the time I got there, with the damage done!"

As it came back to MacLaw afterwards in all its detailed clarity, it was as if the colonel was talking against what was happening; for it was happening all the time he talked, and after it was over, there was no telling when it began to happen or when it ended. It was like a breath of wind through the strung-out camp, with heads coming up to breathe it and one man dropping his meat can and another pointing in idle curiosity to the lone feathered horseman a scant two hundred yards beyond the west-flank sentry line.

The doctor was sure, afterward, that the horseman had been there all the time the colonel talked, sitting his pony against the last of the western light; then raising his brown arm high above his head. The foray cut in at full gallop, coming up out of a draw like prairie wind, pointing for the cattle herd. At first sight of that, you can't believe it, for it's too starkly beautiful, until you know the murder in it. Racing feathery streaks, bunched in a broad arrowhead, with the riders low to the ponies and hanging to the far side. Then it broke into screams that beggared description, for the Plains Indian throws his war cry up from his diaphragm and it comes out of him on a full piston of air, torn not by his lips but curdled in his writhing throat muscles.

There was a scramble of feet, and the colonel, gun whipped out of holster, was racing headlong toward the point of impact with the doctor and Lieutenant O'Hirons at his heels.

CHAPTER FIVE

U NTIL the war whoops tore the air, the infantry outguards just stood where they were, staring open-mouthed at it as if it were part of a play. Then they fired single shots into it that were like the quick ripping of heavy cloth. Fired from the half-ready, without sighting; and the outguard line scattered and went down under the galloping ponies like wheat chaff, with somebody bawling for the corporal of the guard, in a shrill voice on the edge of breaking. *"Infantry's got to fight where it stands."*

Major Ingraham sprinted headlong toward the outguards, empty handed, his looped braces trailing, his trousers slithering, shouting to them to form line, to assemble on him, while trying to hold up his trousers. But there was no maintaining that line, for the flood was full over it now, with Ingraham alone in the path of it, leaping for the head of an Indian's pony as if he would bulldog it off its feet. MacLaw saw the black splash drench the pony's neck as the steel-pipe axe sank in Ingraham's head.

Then for a brief, stark moment the whole thing seemed to stand still, to be caught there before their eyes like a cyclo-rama. There were a dozen men down with Ingraham, and the ponies were surging over them as they clawed up at the hooves with their hands. And the screams stood still in the evening air, hanging in echo that would still be in the ears weeks later when sleep broke suddenly in the dead of night. Then the sharp hooved ponies passed, and there were men in frightful agony where they had been, grovelling desperately to the bosom of the earth, bloody fingers clawed into it, dragging themselves in their broken helplessness, calling in anguish, crawling, dropping back to the ground, rolling over and lying still like torn bundles that had been discarded. All but an arm that kept thrusting up into the air and striking the ground again like a crimson flail. All but one voice that kept screaming insanely, "Oh Christ, *Christ! Shoot me!* Shoot me! Mother, *Mother.* Shoot me. *Shoot me!*"

Colonel Janeway raced through the civilian wagon park, digging his heels in to stop himself, raising his handgun to fire into the face of the charge, as if he were on a garrison range. I Company, of the third battalion, was on the mess line beyond the wide-grazing cattle herds. Women shrieked. A bearded man leaped to the tail gate of the nearest emigrant wagon, long rifle in hand. He fired blind and tore the lower jaw off I Company's quartermaster sergeant. The sergeant's dipper of hot slum spun into the faces of the top men on the mess line, blinding them as the company scrambled for its stacked arms.

Four of the stacks went down, with a thrashing tangle of men on top. The doctor wrested the rifle from the bearded man in the wagon, but there was no time to reload, for the Cheyennes cut through the column hell for leather, stampeding the cattle herd and carrying it with them. For thirty shrieking, shot-torn seconds they were going through in a hoof-thundering roar, then they were gone and there was nothing where they had gone through but a cloud of low dust, the stark echo of their passing and three of them down under the colonel's gun—one under a broken-necked pony.

Then again all of it seemed to stand still for another second, caught in unbelievable shock. The men on the collapsed rifle stacks lay like men thrown from a broken scaffold, stunned to immobility. I Company's quartermaster sergeant lay flat on his back, both gouted hands clasped to what was no longer his face, with the thick blood welling through them and the dreadful bubbling of his vocal cords muffled by them, until he tried to scream—and then the awful sound of that.

The fallen night was full of faces, faces staring open mouthed, with the breathing harsh in throats burned dry. Faces trying to rationalize thought with speaking, but for that shocking moment there were no words, only the breathing in rasped throats and the eyes that flashed wildly like animal eyes in the firelight. Then the words came in a stupid rush of useless orders, in hoarse howls and curses, in senseless ululation, just to make sound and by it to bring some semblance of humanity back into the picture.

Lieutenant O'Hirons was trying to tear the long rifle out of MacLaw's hands, screaming for it, tugging red-faced and furiously in a kind of lurching dance step, his hat gone and his mouth streaming saliva. A white-haired soldier in I Company had a rifle laid across a wagon wheel, squeezing off on it and knocking over a duck each time he fired into the galloping raiders, until they were out of range.

The colonel still stood where he was, clicking his gun twice before he realized it was empty. Just for a flash, then, he flicked it in air, caught the hot barrel and sank the butt of it into the eye sockets of the pony-caught brave. Vicious ax blows, twice. Up and down. Up and down. Like pine wood breaking. Then he dashed across and kicked in the base of the skull of the second, dodged the thrashing knife of the third, wrested it free and cut the sharp blade through to the neck bone. A gout of blood soaked his coat sleeve and glued his face, up into the hair roots.

There was obscenity in the colonel's action, something so unclean, that MacLaw turned his head from the sight of it. It was like a child caught in the frenzy of fury, thwarted somehow and wreaking an untutored vengeance on inanimation. For this old man to do it was as evil as the smell of old age itself. His body bent to it in rigid outline, curved to it like the scythe of death, angled horridly against the night sky. It was a grotesque dance he hurled himself into with cold and ungoverned fury. But there was no symmetry of dancing —a scuttling rather, a scurrying that was completely animal and there was an animal keening in his throat as he killed the three wounded Cheyennes.

Then he stopped with his eyes bone white in the darkness, and he stood hunched and rigid as if the strength had gone out of him with the last of his kill, leaving him still poised in the act of killing, with nothing left to strike into for a revenge that had no meaning now, for the blood that had been spilled and could not be bought back for pain or gold.

Then the colonel swore into the night, and the sound of it was lurid in futility, like words scrawled upon a fence in secrecy to stimulate the thinking into filth.

There was nothing left, but Sergeant Caulter drowning in the thick flood from his severed tongue. Nothing left but the colonel wiping a sleeve to his sticky face and staring in utter disbelief. Nothing left but a group between the wagons around a woman who was shrieking, with the fingers of her right hand dangling from cut tendons like young carrots. Shrieking and flapping the useless hand, as if she would fling it from her and be rid of its crimson horror. Nothing left but a four year old girl in Martha Cutting's arms with a .44 smashed through her sternum. "Indians, weren't they, Martha? Real Indians?"—so softly that Martha had to lean to hear.

There is unspeakable shock to such a thing—the white shock of looking down at one's body and seeing the raw ankle stump of a crushed off foot. Men gaped with their mouths open and trickling. Women whimpered in their throats, and eyeballs dried in their sockets, for the reflex to blink them was temporarily lost. And the shock stayed, it didn't die. It hung over the column like the echo of a beaten gong.

Doctor MacLaw knelt down by the little girl, but he looked at Martha Cutting. There was no color at all in her lips as she held the child's head across her knees, smoothing the damp hair. But there was heat so utterly fierce in her eyes that the doctor looked away. He put his fingers to the little girl's slow heart flutter, and felt it stop. He didn't have to say it.

"And this is what they do?" Martha said.

"That," he nodded, "is what they do." He stood up. Behind him he could hear Mr. O'Hirons shouting to the third battalion to break camp and close up the interval where the herd had been. He could hear Colonel Janeway doubling the outguards and reforming them personally—ordering rifle pits to be dug along both sides of the long bivouac. "Will they come back?" Martha asked. The doctor said, "They do not fight at night, Martha."

She shook her head, tight-lipped. "Will you stay with Nancy until I find her mother?"

"No," he said. "Don't go yet. A little time now is of no importance," and he stood there facing her, his hands upon her wrists. She was rigid, her strong legs spraddled, her head thrust back in militant womanhood, her breasts high and pointed under her bodice. She stood filled with the will to kill, in fierce and silent vengeance, as savage women kill. For it takes far less for a woman to drop the cloak of civilization than it does a man.

She trembled with the turmoil in her, and the color was gone from her face until her features were a gray mask in the darkness. He felt her wrists twist and her fingers claw frantically for his, as if in holding to him she would hold the frightening ebb of humanity that was draining from her.

He clutched her hands and felt hers clutching his. Felt her body thrust tight against him, and then felt the strength leave her until all that held her on her feet were his arms tight laced about her. Her cheek was against his, then buried in the hollow of his shoulder, and the quick flow of hot and silent tears drenched his shirt. And because he was a man wise to life, he held her gently.

The colonel walked slowly back up the column. He was a very old man suddenly, in his shoulders and in his walking. He stopped and looked at MacLaw for a second or two without speaking, as if he were groping for some thought that had slipped his mind, or as if he recognized the doctor's face, but could not quite place him in the scheme of things. His tongue snaked out to wet his parched lips, and then, as if he had remembered, he drew his gun from its holster and reloaded it slowly and thoughtfully, for the hard, firm feel of the cartridges between his fingers.

"I spoke too soon, captain," he said, and MacLaw felt a surge of pity go through him for the older man. *He's run it out. He shouldn't be doing this. He should be jar away somewhere, snug in bed, with all of it behind him.* "Major Ingraham is dead," the colonel said. "My best battalion commander."

In facing MacLaw to say that, Colonel Janeway was facing roughly a little east of south. Something in his eyes made the doctor turn around and look where the colonel was looking. The darkness was full now, and against it there was pink fire glow washing the low clouds, and the reflection traced an arc that curved slightly across their rear. The camp of the tribe migration, twelve miles back of them. There would be hundreds of squaws squatting at the outer edges of those fires, to follow doggedly in the column's trace while the braves harassed its flanks, to cut down stragglers, to loot abandoned wagons. Like a slow flight of buzzards, those squaws, closing in on the rear, waiting for footsteps to falter, to stagger in a circle, to go down. The doctor shivered slightly, for his wet shirt was cold in the night air.

Before moving on, the colonel said, "It's useless to screen me now. Tomorrow give me a rear guard, captain. Cover the column's tail with your troop."

Martha Cutting knelt down and cuddled the dead little girl in her arms and stood again facing MacLaw. The little girl's hair swathed her right arm and hung loose with the firelight burnishing it bright gold.

"Come with me," she whispered, and together they walked into the park of wagons, searching for the dead girl's mother.

"Her name is Nancy Hostetter" as if she would deny death itself. "Go ahead of me and call for Sam, her father. Tell him first."

And afterwards, with the little girl lying as if in sleep on her tiny blanket, Martha put her hand to the doctor's arm and walked with him to the other side of the wagon. There were no words between them, as he put his arm about her again and turned her face up to his. "Martha," he said, "you must not be frightened at what you felt within you. Women out here experience what you felt sooner or later—that there is killing in them as there can be in men. That is why they become excellent shots and as keen to the trail as most men are. It's natural—to this country. It's what will make this country, if it is ever to be made. Remember that."

CHAPTER SIX

THE REGIMENTAL SURGEON, Doctor Haberschaft, was old. He wore a white linen duster over his blue coat, and the lower lid membranes under his eyes were bright wet red in the firelight. He needed a shave. White stubble. And he needed the dust shaken out of his toupee. He was rinsing his hands and his instruments in a horse bucket and looking over his steel spectacle rims at the stretchers about the fire. The thin knife of his chloroform still hung in the wood-ash smoke of the fire. Two stretcher men were carrying Mrs. Omwake back to her wagon, her bandaged hand strapped across her flat bosom.

"Z'voman should get back zum vunction f'om z'vinger tips ewentually. Eight dead. Zix vounded. Vun soldier vill die," Haberschaft told O'Hirons.

Young O'Hirons stood uncertainly in the firelight looking down at the stretchers. He felt an echo of the pain that hovered over them in labored breathing and the soft staccato beat of boot soles chattering against each other in anguished tattoo. It frightened him to see the penalty laid out before him in this fashion, for it had nothing to do with a galloping horse in the dust of the column, with the band music that had sent his boy's brain in search of gold lace and glory. Then suddenly it did. It was a part of the fanfare, and there he himself lay, shattered in youth and helpless. In that moment he grew up, and a furious lash of anger at Haberschaft welled within him. "Who are they, doctor, not just six wounded, like oat sacks. What are their names?"

Dr. Haberschaft looked at him over his spectacles. "Ven vounds oder sickness giffs, it is nod names I am after, but eggsamination for diagnozes und prognozes. Names you get from the Gonzolidated Morning Report, to-morrow, *hein?*"

O'Hirons took a deep breath and turned from him. He walked slowly back toward the C.O.'s bivouac area at the head of the column, with the beginning of wisdom inside him.

The Reverend Tyler Clutterhoe had his people gathered together between the wagons for a burial service, with his great Bible open on a barrel top and a tuning fork in his left hand. An amazingly tall man, the reverend, with a Lincolnian stoop and a beard, the jungle of which could not hide a thundering Adam's apple when he turned his face skyward to talk directly to his God. It went up and down his throat like a fist pounding a lectern, as he shouted the Judgment down upon the savages, as he gave unto God the keeping of a child's soul. "Amen!" he roared, and struck the tuning fork upon the iron tire of a wagon wheel so sharply that the heavy liquid E sang through the night like a beaten sword blade.

Martha Cutting, bonnetted for the service, stood just beyond the firelight, her fists clenched tightly and pressed into her skirts. Doctor MacLaw crossed and stood beside her for the hymn. But she did not sing. She stood there, staring into the darkness beyond the bivouac, her eyes angry flame beneath the shock that still veiled them.

It was in that moment, that MacLaw knew what a woman was meant to be. Not a soft and yielding creature, but a fierce companion in the fight. Ruthless, with no quarter to give when attacked in what was hers. As she looked at him, it was almost as if she were asking him for the blood of vengeance, and she must have seen that in his face, for she said, "You are appalled at what I am thinking? You do not know much of women's minds, do you, sir? Are you not married?"—and her eyes widened in surprise for a moment before the blood suffused her cheeks at her boldness.

"For a few months once. Long ago. My wife died," he said.

She put her hand out with quick sympathy, but she did not touch him. "Forgive me, for I have hurt you."

He shook his head. "No," he said, "the hurt is quite long forgotten," and because there was still embarrassment in the girl, he smiled and said, "And how is the sick man you told me of last night in Cashman's? The man Doctor Haberschaft diagnosed as grippe?"

"I have asked the doctor to see him again. He is extremely ill, I believe. But Dr. Haberschaft is too busy with the wounded." She pushed her bonnet from her head, so that it hung in back from the ribbon about her neck.

"Let *me* see him then."

"But you command the cavalry troop. I don't think you could tell anything more about the man's symptoms than I can."

The doctor smiled again. "Will you be the custodian of a dark and dismal secret?" he asked her. "I am the victim of expediency. There is no one else to command the troop. I am an Army surgeon. Knowing that fact would quite probably kill the colonel of shock. My own men would die of mortification, if the infantry found it out."

She laughed softly. "The secret is safe with me. Will you *please* look at the man then?" They walked back together toward the wagons. She held her great calico skirts in both hands as if they were silk and lace that she would keep from the beaten dusk. An instinctive gesture that women lose quickly on the frontier. "Where is your home, Martha?" Her eyes faltered in sadness, and for a moment she did not look at him. Then she smiled, her lips pressed tightly together. "Since my father died, in that wagon."

He said, "Mine is even less complicated. It is in two straw panniers of medical supplies and instruments, and a rolled blanket up ahead."

Quick laughter was in her eyes. "Then I have been a snob, sir, have I not?" And she half curtsied, so that he saw the clean, straight part in her bright hair.

He was aware again of her intense vitality, as he had been when he lifted her from the broken duckboard walk at Cashman's. A strong girl in mind and body, with the restlessness of life surging within her.

"Worse," he smiled, "for you have been a snob in humility. Only insecure people are humble snobs, defending their right to the lesser things of life as a defense against not having the greater things."

"Which are?"

"Quite simple," he said. "A home place for the chimera of permanence. Security in work, with the promise of tomorrow. Someone to share triumphs and defeats with.'"

"But you have none of those things."

He laughed softly. "That is how I know the truth I speak of. Martha, do you feel as if you had known me for a longer time than you have? A much longer time?"

She stepped slightly back from him, as if he had made to touch her. "Why do you ask that?"

"Because it seems that way to me. It seems as if we had said parts of these things to each other long years ago. As if it was all there in the shadows of memory."

"I don't—know."

The man, Garsten Ott, was quite ill. Doctor MacLaw examined him carefully. A cadaverous man, Ott, drained out by years of dulling labor until his great lank frame was work-whipped to knobby bones and leathery flesh. The doctor had seen it often before, the hard scrabble farmer, fighting the bad land of his own or his father's choosing, clinging to a marginal existence until the dream of the west thundered hope into his dulled brain. Years of clearing the thick grown wilderness, the terminal rock deposit, and the dead heart of the soil itself. Such men died early, for the stamina to coast on in middle years was all burned away in youth.

Ott's wife was his counterpart, a dry woman baked with toil to gray drabness. Her teeth all gone, and she was not yet thirty-five. Her eyes deep with the light of fear and ignorance. It was the diet, at base, that really did for them. They fried everything, filling their systems eternally with thick grease, living mostly on pig and soggy baked bread, draining themselves utterly of any power to resist illness. Kentucky foothill people without the will to climb high into the mountains or the ability to go and live in cities. Caught in limbo, with no hope left in them except the vague and moving western dream that had finally compelled them to pull out their roots, pack their chattels and move out blindly toward its expectation.

Ott was in fever, with intermittent chills and a lethargy that was too deep, the doctor felt, for grippe. There was backache, his wife said. Doctor MacLaw palpated, but there was no pronounced lung congestion, nor had there been vomiting as yet. But just as the doctor climbed down from the wagon with Martha, Ott did vomit.

They stood together at the tail gate, looking steadily at each other. Above them they could hear Mrs. Ott's harsh voice lowered to soothe her husband, hear her cleaning him up. Then she dropped down to the ground beside him and looked full at the doctor.

"Tell me," she said.

"I cannot tell you anything yet," he said. "Except that you must burn that cloth you wiped him with."

"Tell me if he'll die."

Doctor MacLaw smiled. "My dear woman, far from it," he said. "He is a very sick man, but he is far from being mortally sick. You must keep him covered up warmly and give him water when he wants it. Soft foods only, until we know more. Soups and broths. And I will see him again."

"You ain't lyin' to give me hope?"

"I am not lying. And you must not let hopelessness come into your own mind. It takes time to diagnose these things and time to cure them. Keep him as comfortable as you can —and as clean. And let him not worry about himself, for he will if he sees that you worry."

As the woman left them, Martha stepped out to the wagon side and stood there, staring back at the reflection of the Indian camp fires across their rear. The doctor looked down at the scuffed tips of his boots. "And the squaws, I am told, are more savage than the men!" the girl said, and her voice dropped to a whisper. "Have we smallpox, Doctor MacLaw?"

He looked full into her eyes. "You have helped nurse this man, suspecting strongly that we might have it?"

"Come," she said, "I'm not a female scatterbrain. My father was a doctor of medicine!"

He nodded. "There is a strong possibility of smallpox. I tell you that in full professional confidence. These people must not panic, until we know for a certainty. Even then, there must not be panic!"

Martha said, "I have a deep respect for the oath of Hippocrates," but there was no high pride in that; just a plain statement of a manner of living, as if, instead of speaking, she had held out her hand for him to grasp its cool firmness, in quite professional loyalty.

A great comfort came upon him, like warm prairie rain after a long drought, for it is not good to walk this world alone. And he wanted to help her in her worry now as she had helped him with her words. He said, "Martha, the little boy who died at Cashman's. Was he robust in health otherwise?"

She shook her head. "He should never have come with us, poor lad. He had a lame leg from an old illness. And he coughed continually. When"—she nodded toward the Ott wagon—"this sickness took him—if the two sicknesses are the same—he just died."

Fervently, from the preoccupation of his own professional thinking, the doctor said, "I'm very glad of that! *Very* glad," and then realizing what he had said, he looked up at her amused smile of understanding, and met it with a grin. "You *do* know doctors, don't you? Now one other thing. Are there any other children—with even slight sniffles?"

She nodded. "Three or four. There always are, with all the dust we breathe."

"Stay here," he said, and he doubled through the camp to his panniers, made a carbolic wash for himself and for her and came back to look at the children.

When he had finished, he and Martha stood again between the wagons and the newly dug rifle pits. "The children who are well must not go near the children with sniffles until I know what those sniffles mean. Nor the man. Nor must his wife or the children's families mingle with the rest of the people. No one who has not been in contact already must go into the sick wagons or touch anything that has been used by the sick. Anything used must not be strewn carelessly through the camp. It must be safeguarded until day's end, and then buried. You must keep Ott and the children from the cold of nightfall. He must not be uncovered in his fever spells—or must they, if they develop fever. Their bodily functions must be kept to regularity, and their diet must be entirely liquid. I will send you purges for them all. And they must be kept in bed."

"I will see that it is all done," she said, "and how long will it be until we know?"

"There are didactic rules in books,"—he frowned—"that have never interested me too much. One man will observe three days of fever before the papules of smallpox. Another six or even more. For similar diseases they will say fourteen to sixteen days of incubation. And another man will say eight to eighteen. What they all seem to deny is that each patient's constitution is an entity, with its own individual reaction to infection." He, too, now, was looking back toward the reflection of the Indian fires on the distant clouds. "With aboriginal people, for instance, with no race immunity, the white man's illnesses seem to scourge them like prairie fire. And yet we, for all our own barbarity, cannot stand pain as they can. Shall we say, then, a *few* days?"

"Thank you, doctor."

For a moment more, the doctor stood there looking at Martha, and the girl was no longer embarrassed under his direct gaze, for it was as if he were searching his mind for any further instructions that he might have to give her. Within her, there was a pleasant warmth at the trust he was bestowing upon her with an earnestness that took it for granted that she would accept it. Suddenly she wanted to mend the rent in the sleeve of his shirt, and the impulse startled her.

The doctor said, "And for you, you must use the carbolic wash each time you leave a sick wagon. You must not tire yourself unduly nor breathe the breath of patients."

"Is it more dangerous"—she held her head high—"than the air you breathed today with the troop?"

CHAPTER SEVEN

INDIANS do not fight readily at night—for an Indian killed at night wanders forevermore in the darkness beyond the Hunting Grounds—but as MacLaw rolled into his blankets and lay staring at stars so close above him that he could smell their cold ice, he listened acutely to the noises of the night—to a coyote's shrieking laugh and a mourning dove speaking from sleep in a land of no trees—and he knew that the Pawnee, the Cheyenne and the Arapahoe were in close to the camp, singly and silently, scouting the sleeping column with their eyes far enough beyond the fingers of the fires so that no chance gleam would make them bright amber beads in the prairie grass.

He lay long without sleep, rolled in his blankets, thinking the situation out. The Indian mind is very like a child's mind, resisting coercion with an animal's instinct, quick to realize when advantage lies with them, inexorable in forcing it. To them, the huge column of white-eye soldiers had lost face twice with this day. Once with the burning of Cashman's Settlement and again with the failure to stop the sundown foray that cost the cattle herd. So now the chiefs knew the strength of the column, knew that it would not turn back to join battle or stand steady when battle was offered. Knew that it could not. For the rest then, follow the long march day by day, cutting it up a little at a time until the heart of it was dead for the final kill.

The colonel felt it, too, in his own vague way, for no longer did he want his march screened ahead and to the flank, as if he still marched in strength to impose the will of arms. But he wanted a rear guard tomorrow instead, as if he had already accepted the fact that he was running away and must interpose the troop between his path of flight and the steady, plodding pursuit that dogged his tail.

Forsythe's book said: "The object of the rear guard is to check pursuit and thus allow the main body to move unmolested." Doctor MacLaw frowned in annoyance. Precisely the sort of nonsense a man came upon at times in medical treatises, written in pomposity that completely ignored all details. The statement was as sophic as if it had said, "The object of the practice of medicine is to cure the sick," and he had an overpowering impulse to hurl the book from him and scrabble the leaves down the dawn wind. But he didn't. He mounted his horse and passed the rear guard order to Sergeant Elliott.

There was dawn light enough now to move. There were thick mist pools still in the hollows, but straightaway visibility was clear, to four hundred yards. Back of him in the column, Doctor MacLaw could hear the first battalion moving out through the mists. He could hear the company commanders forming column—"Fours! Fours right!"—and the heavy wagon wheels growling in congealed hub grease. The teamsters shouted and cracked their long whiplashes.

He rode slowly along toward the rear of the column, about a hundred yards out from it, watching it get into motion, leaving its fires stamped out to smoking embers and its night litter strewn to either side beyond the camp limits, and the thought was in him that where those seventy-odd people of the Reverend Clutterhoe finally stopped for their last camp, a town would grow, with a church and a school and houses, and he could see it suddenly in the mists, with white clapboards to the houses, a broad main street and yellow window lamps at night. Clutterhoe, Wyoming, possibly, with little girls in pink sashes going to Sunday school, and carols on Christmas Eve. A safe town; not like

Cashman's, but an integral part of the growing states that would some day reach all the way to California.

He wouldn't have ridden in to the emigrant train, if he hadn't suddenly seen the girl Martha again. The wagons there had not got the word to move yet, and she was coming out from between two of them. The doctor swept off his hat. "Good morning," he called.

She pushed her hair back with a quick flick of her hand and looked at him, smiling. Always when she moved that way, there was dynamic life in her whole body. A gentle surge of living that seemed to hold her poised for a second, breathless with the expectation of life. She raised her arm to him, and took several steps toward him, to meet him as he rode in.

"Good news," she said in a low voice. "Garsten Ott spent a comfortable night. There is still fever and chills, but no more vomiting and the children do not appear to be any worse than they were."

"That *is* good news." He nodded. And you? Did you get a good night's rest?"

"Never better," she smiled.

"I shall be at the rear, from now on," he said, "trying whatever we can to discourage the pursuit. But at to-night's halt I will see you."

She nodded, her hands intertwined lightly. "And you will not take unnecessary risks? You will be careful?"

There were bright crimson streamers on the tail gates of five of the prairie schooners—about two feet of narrow cloth tied neatly on the left side. Soft cloth. The doctor took a streamer in hand, fingering it. Martha said, "They are to mark the sick wagons. To keep the well children from them, during halts."

Still fingering a bright ribbon, the doctor smiled. "That is a splendid idea. There must be a strain of savagery in me for bright things always attract me."

"We found a bolt of the cloth," she said.

"If there is enough left," he told her, "it could be cut into squares and made into handkerchief dolls, to amuse the children we are keeping in bed with the sniffles. Would that be a good idea?"

"But of course it would!" she smiled.

The leading wagons began to move with a heavy crack of wheels. "Martha! Climb on!" and whips cracked all along the line.

The doctor walked D Troop in column of twos past the plodding third battalion, now under MacCluskey, its senior captain, and wheeled it into position about a mile behind the tail of the column. They followed on in close order until the day lightened to the horizon and the red rim of the sun set fire to the top ridges of the now-distant Estrellas and flamed in their eyes. For an hour they could not see anything behind them because of the sun, so they rode along at a walk in the column's litter. Broken boxes and rags and barrel staves, then the low mounded graves of Major Ingraham and the eight dead soldiers and the small grave of Nancy, almost as if they were litter now, too. Bits of rope and leather strapping ends. Suddenly a hand mirror and a piece of bright lavender ribbon trampled in the dust, and then the stiff, waxen bodies of the three Cheyennes and the dead pony. A bloody scrap of bandage, a child's paper pinwheel, a new tin dipper and a comb with bright glass jewels set in it. A frayed gallus strap, a pair of spectacles with the lenses gone. And far off to the flank, a white stoneware pitcher. Like a gigantic paper trail the column was deliberately leaving behind in a game of hares and hounds.

Sergeant Elliott's face was clinched in anger. "Fancy-pants recruits! Don't they never police up, sir?"

Still it continued. A bottle with a syrup label, the cover of a school copy book, bits of cloth and, as the morning wore on, a bright red handkerchief doll. The doctor smiled and made to ride over to the flank to pick it up and take it along with him, that Martha might give it back to the child who had lost it. But just as he kicked his foot out of his off stirrup, there was a shout from Corporal Fleming on flank guard. Fleming pointed to the east, and high against the sun on rising ground they saw a party of hostiles sitting their horses, watching the column.

That was all the Indians did for several days—watch. They had what they had come for last night—fresh meat on the hoof, and their lean bellies were glutted. It was almost nine o'clock before the dust of the main tribe migration began to hang high behind the marching column. But when it did, the heavy, plodding pursuit was on full, dead behind today and for all the days to come, closing the distance slowly each day, like the years that march in line behind a man's living, until one day he must stop and lie down and let them march over him.

The doctor estimated five days for the stolen herd to feed the tribes. It lasted six. Six days for foot blisters to form and break and tear and bleed, until feet sucked wet when shoes came off at night. Six days that rasped men's throats with incessant dust coughs and deadened Janeway's regiment, until there was no yesterday distinct from the day before. Nothing but the dread of tomorrow and the empty miles ahead.

The regiment marched in sullen apathy, with the quick, loose grousing gone out of it. And when the men don't grouse, morale is at its last ebb. Officers' faces were frozen in continual silent anger, and the long service non-coms were quick with the ripped curse and the boot toe. And yet where is the blame? A regiment of scattered low-strength companies, suddenly concentrated for the first time in a dozen years and brought hastily to war strength with recruit replacements through the exigency of the frontier situation. No time to boil it down into an efficient team. No time to build the training up the necessary pyramid from the individual to the apex of concerted team effort.

It would be some time in history yet before a fatuous silver-tongued orator would thunder that a million men would spring to arms overnight—before the echo of knowledge came back to him—"What arms—and who feeds them breakfast the next morning?" For it is that way in the United States. No certain conviction that a guard must be placed eternally over it to defend its concept. Instead, an apathy in peacetime, and then the frantic improvisation in time of war to plug a finger into the dike, until sometimes one wonders what careless shoulders the mantle is draped upon.

CHAPTER EIGHT

THERE WAS still no rash on Garsten Ott, the night of the sixth day, and the whole column was sniffling as badly from the dust as the children in wagon quarantine were. Ott was still a very sick man, but there was hope in Martha Cutting's tired smile.

"You must think me an indecisive fool," the doctor spoke earnestly for himself, "but I will not put a label upon a bottle until I know its contents: I am not sure and I cannot speak professionally until I am sure. All I can say is that at this moment I do not know whether the man has smallpox or not. But in twenty-four hours, if no rash, no papules have appeared, I can with definite certainty say it is *not* smallpox. You understand me, Martha?"

She nodded. "One small guess in a progression of careful reasoning can break the entire chain and make it useless."

"Is that you, my dear, your thinking?"

She smiled. "No, it is my father's, put into me. But I believe it fully. He used to say nobody in this world works harder to put himself out of business than a doctor does, and if that is the ultimate goal—to empty his pocketbook and render his own children hungry—then it comes of high inspiration and must be attained to in utter honesty of soul and utter integrity of endeavor. No short cuts. No makeshifts. No conscious carelessness. No guessing."

MacLaw put his hand on her arm. "Until to-morrow then. But we must still expect the worst, you understand? Until to-morrow, you will still be careful about the wastage from the quarantined wagons—the children have dropped some of the dolls and pin-wheels you made. And you must get sleep now, yourself."

"I collect the wastage carefully," she said, "and take it well to the sides of the camp for disposal. I am sorry; I will tell the children," but what she wanted to say to him was, "Be careful back there with the rear guard!"

She watched him walk down through the camp, the firelight glinting on the saddle wear of his boots and on the dull brass of his battered spurs. "Please," she whispered to the dead woman, *"do not have been too beautiful!"*

Early the next morning, the rear guard saw a thin line of galloping brown horsemen cutting in along the east flank to parallel the line of march. The doctor counted over four hundred hostiles making no apparent effort to close the distance. Then, for no reason that he could actually identify in his mind, he turned full about and trained his glasses on the opposite flank of the column. There were galloping hostiles on that side as well—about the same number as far as he could tell at the distance.

He studied both movements carefully through the glasses. They had none of the earmarks of an attack formation. They were strung out along both sides in two thin lines, merely to follow, beyond extreme range. It didn't make sense, for Plains Indians only fight in two ways. If their enemy is compact, they maneuver him into circular defense and ring him round for the slow kill. If he isn't, they raid him, chop off his weakest element and try to wear him down piecemeal.

Then suddenly MacLaw knew what it was; not from his own experience, for he had never encountered it before. But in the north along the old Oregon Trail, they had wiped out the entire MacFadden Expedition when control got away from them. The essence of it was control and they used it to divert the march, to canalize and to force a change of direction into a better position for the final attack.

The doctor licked a finger and held it up for wind direction; then he dismounted and ran his hand through a tuft of grass beside him, feeling for night dampness still, but it was gone from the coarse grass under the sun's heat. The tuft crackled in his fingers. The doctor said, "Nikirk, gallop up the column to the regimental commander. Tell him the Indians are getting hungry again, and that he has strong hostile parties on both flanks today, and tell him to expect them to set prairie fires into the column, if the wind freshens. Sergeant Elliott," he said, "I want a squad far out on each flank, to follow those hostile parties. Send me the corporals."

One was Fleming again. The other was Corporal Jardine. The doctor looked intently at their faces as he would look at faces in a hospital ward. "This thing," the doctor said, "is a delicate mathematical equation. There are forty-five men in this troop now, protecting the rear of six hundred infantrymen and seventy-four civilian men, women and children—against twelve hundred hostiles. The Indians I think are about to become epidemic, and the medicine is inadequate. I expect fever shortly. When it comes, I shall use the old-fashioned method of bleeding." Both corporals looked at him blankly. He smiled. "Get far out on either flank. Watch the wind and watch the terrain. Where the wind comes from, that hostile party will probably use grass fires to harass the column. If they do, we'll use fires against the opposite flanking party, set grass fires on them too. You will have to watch the wind every minute of the day. It will not be enough just to see fires set against the column on the opposite flank. When you see fires set, you will set your own fires against your flank party only if the wind on your side carries down towards it. Make a mistake on wind, and the whole prairie can become a raging inferno with no chance for any of us to survive. If it is possible, the mission is to break your flanking party, so that half of them must move ahead to escape the fires and the other half must turn tail and come back. Divide them with fire. And watch the terrain carefully. If you can split part of them off from the rest, drive them across low country, down a draw, and if you can get a signal to me, so that I can interpose the troop across their line of escape, we can draw our blood." Both corporals grinned. "But," the doctor said, "there will be no fight merely to clear the humors of your bowels for the last six days of dust eating. It will be fire, load, lock and fall back, and hit a man every time you squeeze off. Sergeant Elliott, send a man to the regimental quartermaster train, to cut our reserve ammunition wagon out of line and bring it down here where we can get at it."

The flank squads rode out into position, but there was no wind yet, so the main body of the troop followed the column's spoor all morning, at the walk or dismounted, leading, to nurse the horses.

And while D Troop marched, waiting, Martha Cutting in a wagon ahead, slept the sleep of exhaustion. While she slept, Garsten Ott became suddenly worse. His wife sent for Dr. Haberschaft. Lieutenant O'Hirons came down the moving column with him.

The old German took one look and he said, "Id's *Bladdern! Mein Gott,* you know vot z'voman tells? A poy died in Cashman's last veek!"

"Never heard of Blatt whatever. Give me a plain word to take to the colonel. Not a medical word."

"Smallpox," Haberschaft said.

When the word spread—and it spread like scandal—wagons drew away from the Otts' wagon, until it was left all alone on the east side of the marching line. Captain McCluskey, who commanded the third battalion, drew his column to the left, so that it was not marching directly behind the isolated wagon. The Reverend Clutterhoe clucked his people away from it, like a confused hen.

And directly, the hot prairie wind freshened and hauled around out of the north, and there were sudden bright fire points in the tall grass beyond the column's head, with a heavy smoke pall rising above their widening arc and sweeping down on the line of march.

Doctor MacLaw, four miles from the Otts' isolated wagon, drew out his glasses and trained them on the western flank. He saw Corporal Jardine pirouetting his horse on a slight rise, pointing ahead and waving his arm back and forth to indicate the terrain he was on. And ahead, where the corporal pointed, fire points bit into the dry grass well beyond him, sweeping away from the column.

"All right, Sergeant Elliott! Now we'll bleed 'em!"

The troop had been dismounted, leading to save the horses. MacLaw turned them off the rear of the column and mounted them, leading them at the walk toward Jardine's position, until he was close enough in to it to see what Jardine was trying to indicate. Then he saw it, a long narrow draw coming down toward him from the billowing grass smoke. Jardine galloped in, soot-grimed and red-eyed. "I think we've got 'em cold-tooled, sir. There's a cross draw a mile and a half ahead. Our fires should sweep the west lip of it, if the wind holds. They'll go into the cross draw, find this and come down it!"

"On foot, Sergeant Elliott!"

Elliott boomed it out, "Prepare to fight on foot! Dismount! Horse holders in!"

Three minutes later and the troop was prone in position at the draw's neck.

That was as brisk a fight and as one-sided as you please. The suddenness of the west flank grass fires caught the hostiles down wind and full in the face and drove them back at the gallop—drove them back through the draw, across which Doctor MacLaw had D Troop deployed. He held his fire until the bunched Cheyennes were galloping full in the throat of it; then he pulled the snapper on it and laid half of them in such a thrashing, bone-breaking tangle that the other half of them pulled up on it for a stationary target for just long enough to take the second volley full in the face. It wasn't a clean amputation, for five or six hostiles got out of the mess and galloped away through a cloud of smoke before the flames forced D Troop to mount and withdraw. But clean or not, it cut the heart out of the flanking party on the west.

"Let's you and me go to war together sometime, sir!" That was Sergeant Elliott, screaming at the doctor as he galloped back into the line again with the troop.

While the doctor was bleeding the west, a foray cut in through the east flank smoke pall and snagged out the Otts' wagon. MacCluskey got rifle fire on the raid, but the hostiles hit so suddenly they had the wagon turned off and careening with them at almost extreme range before he could deploy.

Half a mile away, the wagon overturned and its canvas top caught fire from the burning grass. Garsten Ott they dragged out of it and scalped in plain sight of the marching men. They looted the wreck and galloped off, leaving the oxen to scream at the flames until the harness burned through and freed them. One of them had Mrs. Ott by her long hair, dragging her at the gallop, like a thrashing barracks bag. Then the flames swept in, and there was no possibility of pursuit, for the wind fanned in furiously, and the fire was like a great crimson skirt, twirled in fandango until the heat of it beat down the rear of the column like the blast from a baker's oven.

Prairie grass fire is like that. It races out in long clutching fingers, like the breath of the furies, turns in upon itself, suddenly, like a frantic horse, pirouettes in a blinding holocaust of towering, writhing flame, and is gone again in low hung runnels of smoke, after the grass that feeds it is consumed. When it was gone, the Otts' wagon was charred wreckage, and the horses in the burned off harness were blackened hummocks of cooked meat, the smell of them hanging thick in the air, bitter with singed hair.

Twice that day, long arms of raging fire drove the column way out of its line of march, and once it was necessary to gallop the ammunition wagons out to the westward to pull around a fire threat, with the entire second battalion breaking ranks to beat at the flames with blankets, so that the column would not be cut in half by the fire. Three times the advance-guard company was driven in on the head of the march.

By day's end, every face in the column was smoke-blackened beyond recognition, and white ash lay thick on clothing until you could no longer tell officers from men, soldiers from civilians. The prairie was rank desolation, and the bitter stench of dead fire was all there was to the evening air. Fire embers, smoldering on the prairie, ringed the march in a sixteen-mile semicircle, when Colonel Janeway went into bivouac, with only twenty-four miles ticked off behind him, against twenty-seven of yesterday.

The Old Man peeled off his shirt and had O'Hirons douse him with a bucket of water. He towelled the soot from his upper body slowly with a sense of infinite weariness. He cleaned his fingernails with his pocket knife and stared down the length of the halted column. It was going slack on him by the minute, and the time was run out when it could be tightened up by any surface methods. If the will to tighten isn't deeply ingrained, you can pull on the top ropes until you are blue in the face and nothing will happen.

As soon as the word to halt was passed, the men fell out all down the line, sat down or lay down, making no further effort for themselves or anything else. The colonel toyed with the idea for a moment or two of a day's full rest, but rejected it, for he knew that if he ever let the command come to a full stop for a day, it would be almost impossible to rouse them out of it. There was fear in it the way it stood, and he could keep fear on his side, working for him, only if he kept the regiment to the march, inexorably each day, as their only possible salvation.

CHAPTER NINE

A T DAY'S END, the great dust pall of the tribe mass, following behind, was only about seven miles distant when it settled slowly down through the evening air on the Indian encampment. The pursuit was closing in.

That night when Doctor MacLaw walked up to the convoy, he found a great gap in the bivouac, with four redribboned wagons alone in the gap and the rest drawn together up ahead. The edge of Captain MacCluskey's camp was a good sixty yards behind, with a sentry line between.

Martha was with the four lone wagons. She brushed a quick hand to hair that the firelight caught in flaming bronze and told him what had happened. He stared for a moment beyond the line of rifle pits into the mist that lay across the distances. And he saw the long, monotonous way he had come to this point in his life, and a consciousness of useless work and of heavy time was on his soul, unblessed by gentler things.

He looked at Martha again and felt the militant rebellion of youth in her, that eternally beats against the world and the conditions the world imposes, and he knew that the last faint shadow of rebellion was leaving him. In a few years now, he would settle to lonely conformity, accepting the conditions as final, choosing the middle course forevermore. In a few years he would be old and complacent and nothing that ever happened to him again would have the power to hurt him much.

For the first time in years, he felt the tears pooling behind his eyes. For there was no time left to them now. He realized, that as he stood there, he was admitting to himself that he had given up hope. When he realized it, however, the slow anger coiled within him and he knew that that is the one thing you cannot do, give up and welter in self commiseration. And where the tears had been, there was hot shame.

"I will not leave these children and their families." There was quiet anger in Martha's voice. "They are not very sick, and I don't think their sniffles were anything more than dust colds, but we have been isolated because of the fear now of the marking ribbons, and I shall stay with them!"

MacLaw passed a hand slowly across his eyes. "It is my doing," he said wearily. "Did Haberschaft find Ott broken out with papules? He *must* have!"

"I do not know. I was sleeping!"

"Damnation!" MacLaw said. "If I could only have seen him! Now we'll never know. These children I do not think have smallpox, but if Ott had papules this morning, and it *was* smallpox—"

Martha touched his arm. "No," she said. "It is not your doing. Whatever the disease was, Haberschaft *made* it smallpox! The damage is done in fear, beyond all undoing now! The whole column knows it!"

"Martha," he said, after a moment, "you will be alone now with these wagons, except for the thin line of outguards on either side." He put his revolver in her hands. "Keep it with you," he said. "Understand me." He looked into her eyes. "Know what I say. Whatever happens, you must not be taken. That is the rule for white women—out here. There are six cartridges in the cylinder. You must save one of them—"

She held the great gun in both her hands, but she did not answer him. She stood there, her head high, knowing what it was that he was telling her and accepting it. "And," MacLaw said, "you will still watch these children continually for a rash—for papules."

She put the gun in the great side pocket of her skirt.

"It's—it's as if you are saying goodbye to me, Robert. Is that what you are doing?"

He took a step toward her, into the shadow of the wagon. With a quick hand he thrust her bonnet back from her head and pressed his face into her warm hair, put his arms around her and drew her to him. He could feel her whole body tremble against his, and he held her tightly to stop it. Then the eternal flame roared between them, and the night was gone under the stars.

"For if there is no time left to us," she whispered, "we must take what there is. We cannot carry this with us and go apart from each other into nothingness."

"I know," he said miserably, "that we cannot. But somehow now, there *is* time left. In some subtle way, I think we have made time for ourselves. Do you feel that?"

"I don't know." She shook her head. "All I know is that if there is nothing else, you must not leave me."

Far up ahead, they could hear the Reverend Clutterhoe thundering for his God to listen to him, demanding of his God that he grant vengeance. There was a heavy annoyance in MacLaw, for God had walked beside him once or twice in his own living, and the memory of gentleness and peace that had been upon him was a very sacred part of his being. No more than you shouted upon a friend for succor, or paraded a friendship publicly for what it gave you, could you do what Tyler Clutterhoe was doing, without the stigma of black pride and bad manners upon you.

The doctor spoke to Colonel Janeway about the gap in the column. The blood blinded the colonel and his lips trembled. When he could talk he said, "And what about my regiment? What do you suggest I do if they all start to come down with smallpox! The gap stays, with a double file of skirmishers out from it on both sides! That's all I can do!"

As he lay in his blankets, too beaten to sleep, one thing alone was in the doctor's mind. *Nine more days to the Paradise—possibly ten—*"and infantry must fight where it stands." *This infantry must, for it is constrained by order to go from A to B; it will be watched and flanked every foot of the way, to be attacked when the hostiles find it advantageous to attack. To be refused a fight when it occupies advantageous ground itself.*

But there is something wrong with that—as wrong as there was with this illness. There is something not in the book that my mind must grope for and find the answer to. I'll admit the order to join General Cook, and that a fight will steal the march time, but the march time has been stolen all day by the grass fires, and to-morrow, and to-morrow, and to-morrow, it will be stolen again. Tonight the tribes are seven miles behind us. To-morrow they will be only six. The next night their camp fires will be a great glowing ring completely around us. There is a sullenness in our eyes already, laced with helpless anger. The march now is like the labored tolling of a great bell—the monotony of it beating into brains with white insistence. Each day there will be more graves in the column's wake, until the time comes when we stop burying our dead.

But again, and he went over it carefully in his mind, suppose that the colonel should elect to force a fight now? He could go into circle defense where he was and offer fight, but it might not be accepted. The superior force of Indians could ring him statically, camp beyond range, and sit him out until his water and rations were gone. If he turned back and marched down on them to attack them, they could draw off with their horse mobility and lead him on endlessly to exhaustion. Either way, the final issue would be joined with Janeway's people forced to the defensive. It was mathematical, as he had told the corporals the day of the first fires, for there would be no final fight until the chiefs were certain that their own massed attack was capable of completely overrunning the *Pinda-lick-o-yi.* Never, in the whole history of the frontier wars, had the White Eyes had superiority except in their own ability to outthink the savage.

MacLaw beat the ground helplessly with his clenched fist.

"Infantry must fight where it stands," but a careful cavalry commander will exploit his mobility to the fullest. Then it was that he knew the answer. And the answer was D Troop. He must continue to use the troop as he had used it the first day the fires were set upon the column—with cunning and subterfuge—to hack the pursuit down, harass it, cut its strength. If each day he could cost the tribes more blood than they took from him, the balance of strength would shift to Janeway's side of the ledger and there might be no final fight.

Hanging back as he was doing now, a rear guard, he was remote from the colonel each day of march, so that local decisions could not be referred. He could make them himself on the spot and take the responsibility and censure later. Further, in the rear guard position he had the initiative always, for each day when the march of the column started once more, the Indians, breaking their own camp and continuing the pursuit, had to fend out and come down upon his own march to make contact once more. If he saw to it that they were off balance when they made that contact, he could bite them hard.

When the march got underway the eighth morning, the doctor held D Troop standing to horse until it was well behind the column's dust-coiled tail. Then he had them lead at the walk through the camp area. It was littered on both sides again as it had been each day before, as if litter was the inexhaustible item of supply the regiment had available. He knew that within an hour, the hostiles would be combing the old camp site like the curious scavengers they were, as they had undoubtedly combed it each day since Cashman's.

Sergeant Elliott jumped off his horse suddenly and snatched up an infantry rifle from the ground. His face was livid as he held it out to the doctor. "Forty-four seventy-four. Some chowderhead recruit throwing away his gun! If he wore spurs, I'd spread-eagle him face down under a wagon-box, sir!"

But Colonel Janeway beat Elliott to it. He had the wrists of seven stragglers lashed to the tailgates of escort wagons before that day's march was two hours old.

CHAPTER TEN

THE EMPTY rifle pits of last night's outguards gaped in the prairie in two long rows like shot holes in dead flesh.

Doctor MacLaw chose the pits that had been dug in an arc across the north end of the camp, for this morning's bleeding. He halted the troop. "I want to lie doggo, dismounted, in these forward pits, Sergeant Elliott, with the horse-holders and the mounts and the ammunition wagon masked in that hollow just beyond. You remain with them, watching me. No matter what force the Indians reconnoiter in, I am counting on surprise to cut a wad of them down, to disorganize them. Your job is to get the troop out of the pits and mounted for the getaway, before they can reform and ring us."

Sergeant Elliott looked sideways along the line of rifle pits, and he stood in his stirrups to look beyond towards the draw. He spat a long streamer of brown juice that slapped into the dust like a thrown cartridge. "It's risky, Cap'n, but I won't say it can't be done. Got to be timed though, to the split second."

"You see that it is," MacLaw told him, and led down into the draw and dismounted the men. He gathered them in and told them all what he had in mind, and then, close to the ground and crawling, he led the dismounted troop back to the rifle pits. The horse-holders in the draw behind, took their shirts off to smother whinnies. And Elliott, halfway between pits and the draw lip, took up his own position where he could see both parties and wait for the signal to come in at the gallop. There is nerve wrack in that, and cold oily sweat in the armpits. You cannot breathe except in the tops of your lungs, and where the hot coffee was in your belly there is nothing left but a round void of emptiness.

The gray dawn light turned to phlegm yellow, and suddenly there was a small hostile scout party riding in to where the lower end of the camp had been. Several of the Indians threw off their ponies and went over the ground on foot, searching it. More came in from the mists, to comb the debris for childish loot, until they were almost like a soldier police detail, spread across the width of the abandoned bivouac and moving up through it toward the troop's position. Presently they were close enough for the men to hear their ragged, throaty talk, so that each trooper in the pits could track his man in his carbine's sights. You could smell them, before the doctor rose and slapped his hat into the dirt for the order to fire.

The first volley bit into the Indians like a hay scythe. One of them galloped headlong into the position and sprawled at a pit lip, his pony thrashing clear over the pit on two broken forelegs. The second volley took them knotted together, the dismounted scrambling to horse, the mounted wheeling to dash out of range. The third was long range, as they re-formed and, on its echo Sergeant Elliott dashed in with the horse-holders, the troop flung on and tore northward toward the distant column.

The running mounted fight lasted twenty minutes, with the troop, as foragers, in a half-circle around their careening ammunition wagon, and the hostiles in two long arms of galloping horsemen, trying to circle them and cut them off. It wasn't clean. Bledsoe, MacKenzie and Halliday lay out behind it, stripped presently, and pincushioned to the ground, staring at the morning sun with eyes that did not see it. Gottschalk, his horse killed under him, ran frantically at Sergeant Elliott's off stirrup leather until Fleming caught a free mount for him. Jardine was drilled through his left side under the short ribs, and four troopers were slightly cut up.

Forty-one men for duty after they got Jardine into the ammunition wagon. Twice surprise had worked, but the hostiles would watch for it now, circle any suspicious terrain, hold off to the flanks until they got their own sure odds in their favor.

But the troop knew its worth and rode in the knowledge of it, knowing the doctor had the answers somehow, even if he didn't have the words of command. Figure the casualties any way you wanted to, but they still stood about eight to one so far. If the whole squadron was along on the party, they could take every man jack of the hostiles and lay 'em in rows like cut wheat, because this MacLaw character had the knack of it, the ability to call the cards. It's something more than the book; it's a knowledge of how an Indian thinks, and the ability to work him around so his own thinking fools him. It's how to use terrain for yourself, and just how far to work the tools you've got to work with, without botching the job or ruining them.

They liked him. He gave them back their pride. They trusted him. And they watched him narrowly, for what was in his mind to do next, for there was no reckless impulse in the man, no risk he didn't calculate to a hair. They knew that that was all on their side.

There were no grass fires that day, and presently they knew why. The fires had burned off the forage and the tribes carried none. So they had to hold off on the fires to feed their own ponies. After the ambush, they were chary of the moving column, for they feared another ambush on its flanks. Further, the column worried them, for it presented no fighting position. If it would go into a defense circle, it could be held static and ringed. But it kept moving, and it kept four and a half miles long without its stolen herd, offering nothing to attack, but its long flanks, with their double line of foot skirmishers out from it on either side.

The hot hours came down full and there was no ambush, so the hostiles closed the distance to the outguard files and, at half past ten that morning, they cut in from the sun with howling fury. About five hundred of them, pointing for the emigrant wagon train. As they came screaming down on the column at full gallop, it looked like the real thing. Captain MacCluskey, who had the Milk Battalion, deployed I, L, M and K Companies at the double, as skirmishers to meet it, fanning them out along the line of outguards to protect the emigrant wagons, to save them from being cut out of line as the cattle herd had been. But the foray turned to parallel the line of march just as it came within medium range, and turning, fired into the troops and circled off again in shrieking derision.

Those hostiles hadn't seen infantry out there since their fathers were strong. And what they had seen so far engendered scant respect, and they showed it. MacCluskey burned eleven hundred rounds of ammunition at galloping targets—and damned poor results from the shooting, for shooting is never a gun and ammunition. It's those hours on the garrison short range. It's breathing and squeezing and the red-necked sergeants bulling it to perfection. Then it's the long range, with the naturals coming out ahead and the rest of the command getting close to possibles, but not quite in there for the top pay. For shooting is big business in the infantry, and it's mass-produced, and if a regiment hasn't had time to get it, God help the regiment when it goes for record.

But this was far worse than poor shooting. The whole battalion had been hoaxed, outthought and out-maneuvred. The Indians had worked them over and they knew it, threatened them, to draw them out of line, to deploy them in a defensive position and draw their fire. Then when it came, they deliberately refused the target, drew off and thumbed their noses. And they were still thumbing them as the battalion re-formed in close order and wheeled back into march line.

The awful thing about it was that MacCluskey knew, and the non-coms knew, that each time they did it again, the same thing would have to happen. The threat would have to be met, because the first time they failed to meet it by deploying, that time the foray would cut straight through the column, carrying everything in its path with it. It meant that from now on the whole command was faced with the possibility of continual deployment throughout the daylight hours, doubling the usual march exhaustion of the men at day's end, and cutting the distance marched by half.

The Indians took to close feints all along the line to draw fire. All afternoon they rode in along the column to right and left taunting it, teasing it, reviling it and drawing sporadic fire. Four times again, part of the column was forced to deploy to meet them. None of the forays cut in through. They came down at full gallop to short range, dusted up the long line with Winchester fire and circled off, screaming in derision. D Troop met the rear forays, until they stopped hitting the rear. At day's end, the column had reeled off a scant twenty miles only, and nine men were dead, with twenty-seven wounded in the whole command.

And at day's end, there was another problem. Ammunition. It was in long supply for the march and the campaign to come, but this new tactic was burning it up and burning it with scant result. The word was passed that fire would be held from then on, until the range was closed to minimum. That meant that you had to bring recruits up onto line and hold them there, loaded and locked, and that's tough on long service troops. It meant that the trigger happy boys wouldn't be able to stand it, and it meant, too, a risk of the line being overrun, or of breaking under the strain and running itself.

That night Colonel Janeway walked back to D Troop's bivouac behind the third battalion, and laid the whole thing before MacLaw in blasphemous syllables. "The bastards have pulled a monkey out of the hat and they know it and I know it." The Old Man wiped his face and neck with a filthy handkerchief. "They can keep this thing up until there's nothing left of any of us. Part of it I can control. To-morrow I shall change the march formation, so that the men won't be run ragged as they were to-day.

"I'm putting the entire regiment into two columns, one on each side of the wagon convoy, in column of fours with the advance guard company to close the forward end and your troop to close the rear. That'll save this eternal time-killing deployment. But it won't save ammunition. If they come into close range, we've got to lay fire on them, but for every one we get at the gallop, we're firing twenty to twenty-five useless rounds. And that's got to stop." The Colonel stuffed his handkerchief back into his pocket. "It's got to stop because ten days of it, if it's continued, will spay my fire power completely!"

"It's an old trick of theirs," MacLaw said.

"I've got a few old tricks of my own," Janeway told him. "It may be that the theory of infantry against cavalry has to be entirely recast. On the march, it seems so. You can't meet mounted raids with foot soldiers, if the raids refuse you a gunfire fight at the last moment. Trying to, only makes a fool out of a man. If you're holding a position with infantry, no cavalry in the world can sabre you off it or shoot you off it. But if you are forced to a continuing march, horse mobility and harassment can cut you down to a nub, eventually."

"Yes, sir."

The colonel looked at him. "But I bought my life insurance in advance," he said. "I bought a troop of horse to screen me. Horse against horse is the answer, and I wish to God I'd asked for a squadron!" He put a hand out and clamped his fingers tightly on the doctor's upper arm. "I want these forays stopped, MacLaw. Stop them! Ride close in to my rear. Watch both flanks and gallop the troop to the point of impact. Stop these damned raids on me!"

For a moment, MacLaw couldn't answer him; then he said, "You know what that means, sir. It means that though I have inferior man power, you are still taking my last weapon from me, surprise. It means they will always see me coming and as soon as they know that I will come, they'll pick the best terrain for themselves and the most disadvantageous for me. It can't last long, for I haven't the men."

"You make it last!" Janeway thundered. "Either you're a cavalry officer or you're not. If you are, act like one. It's a function of cavalry to protect the march. Protect it then and stop these raids!"

"And who will stop them for you when the troop is run down the drain, sir?"

"Damn your eyes, MacLaw. I'm not in the habit of having my orders questioned or of entering into debates with my officers when I give an order! You've heard the order. Carry it out!"

"Yes, sir."

And so it was, and each day the troop's Morning Report held less names for duty and the Horse Book was checking the mounts off almost as fast.

It must have been the eleventh or twelfth day that the troop ran itself down almost to a dead stop. The hostile flank parties were far stronger that day than they had been any day before. Their long brown parentheses bracketed out on both sides, as soon as the sun was up, and they rode stolidly just beyond extreme range. Twice before the noon halt, they knifed in to hit the tail of the column hard, but the flank squads of D Troop spotted the assembly points and the troop still met the raids, paralleling them, drawing them down into the infantry rifle fire, driving them off. "Otway, Dannecker, Forbes and Gottlieb from Duty to Killed in Action." Storrs, Jacobus and Tilton in the escort wagons with wounds. Thirty-four for duty, and six led horses on. halters at the tail gates, whimpering at each shot, rolling their eyes white, tugging and lashing hooves at each other.

There were four more heavy raids in the afternoon and D Troop was pumped, horse and man, with Gottschalk's right thigh torn wide open from knee to hip. Storrs dead of his wound in the wagon, and Holmes, Nethersmith and Corporal Fleming missing after the last afternoon fight. Thirty-one for duty and eight led horses. And at three-thirty, the wind freshened in the north and the column fought fire again for the last three hours of the movement, until the prairie was cindery desolation once more, and men marched with socks tied over their mouths and noses, and the teamsters fought their frantic animals with blood-sodden whips.

When MacLaw drew in behind the infantry outguards that night, he felt the sands of the troop running out fast, felt it in his own heavy fatigue. Sixteen trail-wearing days behind them, horse and man, almost two weeks now of this detail and a thirty-three percent casualty list on top of it. You can talk discipline until your face is blue, but no outfit can take a deal like that. The best won't break, but they fade out standing. And it's the same thing. They'll move out until the last, it's only a few impotent steps, for cussedness and pride.

He looked into the soot-smeared faces and saw it in the men's eyes—anger and weariness, murder and the deep tears that never reach the eyes. They were frayed to a point of being ragged, filthy to a point of being foul, and there was a panicky herd nervousness in the horses. Flanks twitched in muscle ripples and heads tossed up and the unrest of the led horses was in the duty horses. They whistled and screamed on the picket line in long whinnies and bucked and lashed, and it took four men and the farrier sergeant to get a new shoe on Herman's off fore hoof, and Herman had thirteen years' service.

Sergeant Elliott looked at the doctor, and something passed between those two men that would live in both their minds for as long as they lived. You may not speak of friendship or of trust when you talk that sort of thing, for they are peaceful words. There is a hot and vicious love that grows between men in battle—a fierce love that has no place in words or in hand-clasps or in gestures. A part of the soul goes out, and forevermore it is gone. Years and years afterward the first word is "Wasn't that a night!" and they are back at once in the bloody agony. "We'll need an oat issue tonight, sir," Sergeant Elliott said. "A good oat issue, sir."

That night the Indian camp was less than five miles behind them, when the glow of many fires washed rose-pink across the belly of the clouds.

MacLaw walked slowly up to the wagons as he had each night to see Martha, but this night his mind was gone in utter defeat. When he found her, there were no words in him, but she could see his thinking in his eyes and there was no need for words. She took his hand and held it tightly in both of hers, then she led him away from the sick wagons. They went into the shadows beyond the cook fires.

In some women there is an instinct for the eternal function, a knowing deep within that a man must come to a woman in his hour of travail and hold close to the eternal well of life. That it is the full sweep of the cycle of progression from birth to death. That this is all that makes it bearable, and that immortality is its only grail. They sat down against a tiny rising hummock, and MacLaw lay back against it in complete exhaustion of spirit, his arms flung wide and his face gray to the breathless stars hanging close above.

There was a groping within Martha for words now, but they would not come to her lips. For a long time she sat rigidly beside him, her back straight and her hands clasped tightly, pressed into her close pressed thighs. Beyond the line of outguards, there was no to-morrow, nor was there any tomorrow down the long march ahead, for there would be no march now, no ending but tonight. But it was not the barrier to time that held her slow thoughts. It was the quiet knowledge that this tired man beside her was all she had ever lived for and all she ever would live for.

She turned to him then and put her hand gently to his face, and all of her being flowed through her flesh toward him. For a moment he did not move, then his arm behind her touched her shoulders and turned her toward him. He pressed her down until both their bodies sprang together in eagerness and strength. There was silver light in it and a sanctity that blinded them and held their breathing. He tried to speak then, but she put her fingers to his lips, pressed them into his lips, forcing them to silence. They clung to each other in hot and awful tears, knowing that the gods had given both of them the accolade and then snatched it back behind the black curtain of no more time.

A frenzy came upon them with the tears, a blind and hopeless rebellion, and it was as if each of them would deny the knowledge in the other, and when it roared to crescendo there was nothing left to them but man and woman primeval.

MacLaw put both hands to his face and thrashed his long body back from hers, half turning to his elbow, but she drew in her knees, twisting her fingers into his shirt, until he turned again and drew her across him in the starlight, her hair cascading across his grimy face, the tumult of her pounding into him with an insistence that knew no other answer. *It does not matter. We are both so very small now, that nothing will ever matter but what we are to-night!*

Her face was below his then in the starlight, and he could see her lips half parted, waiting breathlessly for his answer, see the ripe beauty of her girlhood asking, asking. And the flame billowed hot between them, exploding into the crimson pillar, and nothing else was left, but the hot and secret flow of immortality that passed between their thirsty bodies on that lone and awful prairie.

Long afterwards, she touched his lips again with her fingers and whispered to him, "No words even now, Robert. Nothing but what we are, what we have made each other be, for that is all I'll ever want. If it must be that you shall die and I shall live, then I shall have you still, in memory. And if I shall die and not you, then you will remember me—always."

He could not answer her, but as he lay there beside her in lassitude once more, he knew somehow that there would be a way out. There was strength in him once more and the great and spreading calmness of body peace. It was as if before this night there had been nothing really in him to push himself for, no real goal worth the full fight. But now there was, and the knowledge filled his consciousness.

He knelt above her and pressed his lips to her forehead. "Martha," he whispered, "there can be no dying—there will not be. Believe anything in your heart, believe it fully, and it *must* come true. For that is what man is, the one animal able to rule himself by his thinking—or destroy himself. Come"—he reached for her arm and raised her to her feet—"for to-morrow we try the fight *again!*"

"Robert"—her face was tilted up to his—"for all my life."

"And for all of mine."

CHAPTER ELEVEN

THE NEXT NIGHT the whole regiment knew the answer. It was in the eyes of the men in the third battalion as MacLaw passed through their area after they halted. You could smell fear through the sour sweat, through the bitter smoke and the hot brown slum. It stalked like a gray beast.

Captain MacCluskey grabbed MacLaw's arm, "You've served out here. What's the answer?"

MacLaw looked at the captain's holstered gun. "That's the only answer," he said, "as long as you can use it. The regiment's got a march order. It marches, the colonel says."

"It can't," MacCluskey said. "We've got to stand and fight! This can't keep up; the regiment's lost forty-five men killed and wounded. If you've got any influence with the Old Man, put it to him!"

MacCluskey was not a boy with the thirst for glory still unslaked. He was a man grown and hard grown and a soldier seasoned the long way. He stood there in his broken boots and his worn and march stained uniform watching the doctor's eyes.

"Damn the man who ordered us into the field in this condition," he said coldly. "Damn him to utter hell and damn his offspring! This has been a good regiment and a proud one, but you cannot race an untrained horse. We needed time, but the only thing left now for us is a fight—and to win it!

"The Old Man will not listen to his company officers, but he'll listen to you. Tell him this. Tell him to let my battalion rest until midnight, and then I'll strip them to light marching order and countermarch them muffled, back to the Indian camp, and shoot the hide off it! I can do it with controlled fire, but even if we are cut to pieces doing it, at least there'll be enough damage done to free the march and let the rest of the convoy get away unmolested."

There were tears in MacCluskey's eyes.

At the head of the column, as it halted for the night, Major Irish had his own personal answer. There had been a gray vortex, for years, in the brain of Major Irish. A dark hole with steep sides that shook him to the core when he peered warily down them, for he knew that some day he would lean over and look full into its bottomless depth, and that looking full would steal his balance and catapult him headlong. He was afraid of that pit when the drink flowed out of his raw nerve ends. But never before had he been afraid of it sober and in broad daylight.

When the column halted, the fear struck him in the face, in the whole body, with the impact of cold mountain air. It was completely from beyond his will, and he could do nothing about it. A Company was marching back in from advance-guard duty. B Company was falling out under arms. Major Irish drew his revolver with a hand that held no feeling. He raised it slowly and closed his mouth over the hard muzzle end. He saw the soot-blackened face of Colonel Janeway staring at him, but it shattered into darkness before the mouth spoke.

The Old Man stood looking down at the body, flung in wreck-age like a stain against honor at his feet, and it was as if Irish had stolen something from all of them. Some decency that they all had had, but had no longer. For that is what self murder does. It buys surcease in black oblivion and denies tomorrow's right to fight, and all tomorrows forever. But the cost is the memory of friendship, for now it could never again be Winslow Irish of

Cerro Gordo, Irish of the Chancellor House Fight, top man of the class of Eighteen Fifty. It could only be Winslow Irish, who shot himself in the mouth on the march to join Cook. Because in all its shame of letting go, that shot from his own gun that blew his head apart was now the one important deed of the major's entire scheme of living. Yes, I remember the name. Winslow Irish. Whatever happened to him, finally? and then the answer. He shot himself. Blew his head off out West. Had Janeway's first battalion at the time.

As Doctor MacLaw walked slowly up through the bivouac to see the colonel, the town of Clutterhoe, Wyoming was no longer standing in the mists of his mind, with its white clapboards and its church steeple and its little girls in pink sashes. It was gone completely, and where it might have been, there was merely a long and empty road, connecting two other towns, with two other names, still to be given them.

There were eight isolated wagons, with Martha shunned by the rest of Clutterhoe's convoy, parked in a circle around two small fires, with a wide gap north and south of them, and only the rifle pits on either side at night and the lines of skirmishers by day to make them a part of the march at all. The sun was gone, but the high afterlight washed the bivouac and the vast and empty distances beyond. There were a few grim civilian men with rifles—a pitiful handful guarding the sick and their families.

Martha said, "The fear is so great now, Robert, that the slightest fever or chill, the slightest cough or sniffle and that wagon is forced to join us here."

"And there is still no rash on anyone?"

"Still no rash. Could it possibly have been smallpox with Garsten Ott?"

"It could have been," he nodded. "Only Haberschaft knows that. I do not think it can be smallpox with these people though, for too long a time has elapsed, we hope. But we cannot know that either, for our possible starting point for incubation is still the dead boy at Cashman's and we are not sure what he had! If he did not have smallpox, our starting point may be Garsten Ott. So you must still admit a possibility of smallpox and you must still watch for papules to appear."

It was a miserable thing standing there talking this way with people around them watching them, but there was nothing else that they could do. The girl smiled at him and brushed her hair back with that quick flick of hand, and there was a vibrance in her whole body as she stood there that drew his soul to her. He thrust his hands deep into his pockets. "Martha," he said, "you have a little dust of freckles across the bridge of your nose, a little dust of golden freckles. Do you know that?"

Colonel Janeway lay flat on his back on his one blanket, seeing again what he had seen in the eyes of Major Irish when the column halted, and wondered what it was in a man like Winslow Irish that could make him quit the job. Seeing back through all of his own years to the times he might have quit himself, but knowing that such a thing was not in him. Knowing now that he must continue the march without a single experienced battalion commander behind him. He smelled of fire, like a singed blanket, and he smelled old, and the weariness of the damned was stamped deep in his blackened face.

He opened his rheumy eyes and stared at MacLaw for a second before he recognized him. Then he thrust himself up and sat braced on his hands. "I've got fifteen malingering recruits lashed to my wagons. I've lost better than a company killed and wounded. The blind fear of smallpox is rotting the whole command. *What trouble do you bring me!*" Red fury darkened his face as he glowered at the doctor.

The doctor was ragged, with his left knee burst out of his trouser leg and one spur gone. His shirt was thick with sweat and dust and soot and body grime, and it stuck to him like a lymphatic scab on burned flesh. The sleeve of his jacket was torn loose at the shoulder seam, and his weariness burned in his eyes. He said, "I don't tell you this until I have to, sir. But I have to now, so you'll know. There is one more day left in D Troop. At to-day's rate, to-morrow night will see us run down the drain, sir. The edge has gone out of the men and the mounts. Our casualties are crowding fifty percent now. I don't know how to put it to you for what it really is, but you must have seen it before in your service."

The colonel grunted. "Yes," he said, "it happens. God's teeth. Everything happens. I'll be down to see the men later to tell them how well they have done. But it won't help much, will it?"

"No," the doctor shook his head. "Not much, sir."

Colonel Janeway stared off toward the outguards, fighting himself inside, kicking at the inevitable.

"I knew you were taking a lacing, but I didn't know you were run out! Well, don't stand there chewing your beard! What do you suggest?"

The doctor squatted down and smoothed a place on the burned off ground with the flat of his hand. He drew a cross. "Cashman's," he said. Then he drew a line north from the cross. "I figure we've marched about two hundred and eighty-five miles, sir."

The colonel pulled a dog-eared note book from his shirt pocket. "Thirteen days," he said, "and by the quartermaster's wheel measurer, I have it at exactly two hundred and eighty-two miles, corrected by dead reckoning for the times the escort train was forced to gallop out of column."

Doctor MacLaw nodded. And for a moment it was as if the bone weariness within him would not let him go on.

The colonel shook him roughly. "Get on with it! Don't go to sleep!"

MacLaw pulled himself up and smiled. "Oh yes, sir. Now then, sir, when were you through this country last?"

"Not since before the war. Why?"

"Well, about twenty miles ahead of us, there should be a series of small terminal moraines—rising ground with rounded tops. They call them The Mounds."

MacLaw spoke slowly, trying to conjure the picture of the terrain back into Janeway's mind from the long years before, and suddenly he saw the light of memory in the colonel's eyes. "Yes, I remember. Of course. It was Eighteen Fifty Two. No, *Three*. I went through here with Charlie Brabacher. Charlie was killed at Thatcher's Island. Of course. The Mounds. But that's not what Charlie and I called them. Did you ever hear the limerick about the young man from St. Kitts'?"

With old minds it is always best to let them wander around in memory until they are done with it and come back to the matter in hand. That way you don't force them beyond capacity. The doctor listened to the limerick, and then after the colonel's roar of laughter died, he said, "The Indians won't let you through there without inflicting terrible casualties on you. The Mounds can mask an attack, and the hostiles can come downhill on you, close in. But if you get into position there first, sir, across the tops of two or three rises, the hostiles can't get through *you*, without coming full into your fire."

"Twenty miles," the colonel frowned. "Is there water in there?"

"Yes, sir, but the catch is you've got to go tonight."

"Why in hell do I have to go tonight?"

"Because if you wait until tomorrow, they'll ride around you and get there first, and be in position to stop you. They know they're near the Mounds, too. They will have been thinking of catching you and finishing you there, for days now."

The colonel didn't answer him. He sat there, leaning back heavily on his gnarled hands, an old tradesman, sound in his years of the craft, but lost to ready facility in it by age and his roaring arteries. There was almost pleading in the colonel's eyes, as there is at times in the eyes of the very sick. A pleading for hope, and it is an old sick-room trick to play for that, to get it on your side. The doctor didn't let him speak. He said, "You've got to go tonight, sir, and you've got to make them believe you're still here. Their night scouts will be in on us again after full dark, and you can't simulate a long, narrow column camp. But you can simulate a defense circle. And when they see it, they'll believe it, if it's well acted out, because they've been expecting a defense circle, hoping for one, ever since we started. Waiting for it, for days. That's all they understand, for that's their one sound tactic." The doctor was pleading now. "Take the hoops and wagon covers off all the wagons and set them up in a close circle beyond the fires. Unload all excess baggage and stack it between. Jettison the tents—"

The colonel fought back suddenly. "My company commanders have signed for those tents; they're responsible—"

"Never mind the tents, then, but the hostiles must believe that circle contains your whole regiment—until you get to the Mounds. They've got to believe we're all here, until you're in position, or they'll get ahead of you and cut you off."

"You can't make them believe it, with only D Troop!"

"No, sir; you'll have to leave me a battalion of infantry."

"A battalion! Are you mad? How'll I get that battalion back? You're asking me to divide my force, MacLaw!" The anger was back in full flood. "Do you think I'm a harebrained yellow leg? Do you think it's Custer you're talking to? This is an infantry regiment!"

The colonel thrashed up to his feet—the blood pounding in his head, his arms flayed out from his sides as if to balance himself. He stood there completely helpless in his dilemma, fighting it with writhing lips and clawing fingers. And all of the past surged up out of him in broken words as he fought himself blindly for a decision. "At the Washita, Colonel Custer—and damn all brevet ranks—divided his force and lost heavily. He did it again at Big Horn, and lost everything. That's why we're here tonight!" And the doctor knew if he said, "Sherman got through Georgia, sir, separated from Grant," the colonel would drop dead.

Finally, Janeway said, "I'll get out tonight, at first dark, and I'll give you two companies, if you'll tell me how you'll get them back to me!" Colonel Janeway was slamming a black fist into the palm of his spread left hand. "They can't march out in daylight without being cut to ribbons. They haven't got horses to ride. Tell me! Tell me how you'll get them back to me! It's all right for your precious D Troop —they can ride—but what about *my* men?"

The were standing slightly off to one side of the beaten line of march, with MacLaw facing down the bivouac, looking across the colonel's left shoulder into the park of the regimental quartermaster train. Just as he reached out to steady the colonel on his feet, an escort wagon lashed sideways and upward, spinning its wheels far out across the burned prairie, dissolving into flying splinters and torn white smoke. Without a sound, for the space of the doctor's blinked eyes. Then a slatting, collapsing roar echoed up the camp, but not alone, for the sound repeated itself again and again like blurred minute guns, and the escort-wagon park was torn asunder in smoke and soaring canvas wagon tops and more wheels and jagged splinters and a squib of an ammunition box flying high on a wide arc and spitting fire and shots from it like a thrown packet of crackers.

Suddenly the doctor began to laugh. It was as if the fatigue riddled fibre of his body had to let go completely so that there was nothing left but laughter. He took Forsythe's book from his pocket and shook it in the colonel's face, still laughing outrageously; then he arched his arm and hurled the book from him as far as it would go, and it struck beyond the burned and beaten dust and broke its binding, fluttering its leaves down the evening wind.

"Wagons!" he shrieked. "I'll get your men out in wagons!" The colonel thrust him aside with one thick arm, as if he were a madman, and stood there motionless, watching the full catastrophe, until the last sound of his exploding ammunition echoed into silence.

He stood there, his shoulders slumped, his great hands dangling at his sides, his breathing deep and labored as if he had run a long race and lost it. And there was nothing that either of them could say. It is always what you have to do laid against the facilities you have to do it with. It is only the method of doing it that is left to the commander's discretion. Never the right of refusal of the mission itself. With the means curtailed, the method must be altered, but the mission must be accomplished regardless. You *will* march to the Paradise and join General Cook. You *will* march to the Paradise, on foot, against overwhelming mounted enemy force. You *will* march to the Paradise, with a full company dead behind you from the harassing action of repeated raids, escorting a helpless civilian caravan as you march. You *will* march to the Paradise with the livid fear of smallpox eating your guts. You *will* march to the Paradise with your ammunition train blown to hell and thunder before your eyes!

You never know how those things come about, unless there is a direct chain of evidence left, and there seldom is. The guard detail around the ammunition wagons was strewn headlong across the blown-out ground where the wagons had stood, like tattered blue bundles of filthy hospital laundry, insecurely tied. A trailing rope from a wagon cover possibly, tarred and lying close to undetected cinders in the burned-off prairie. A spark up the rope, and the ten years of deterioration of that ammunition—stored since Appomattox—did the rest. One wagon let go and the other nine went off in sympathy. And to high hell with a court of inquiry, while a spayed regiment of infantry stands there looking on, with its mouth open.

Five hundred and forty men carrying twenty rounds of ammunition each, in their belts, and not another cartridge to be had for gold nor honor this side of the Paradise River. Thirty-five minutes of a regimental-fire fight left to them. About eleven thousand rounds of ammunition. Say it that way and it's a lot, but say that recruit training is only half finished and that the regiment averaged one sharpshooter and three expert shots per company, and nothing lies between it and a death warrant but fixed bayonets.

But as it can happen at times, that took all of the hot blood out of the colonel and he stood there cold, with the slowness of age stripped from his mind and the sharp blade of what it had been once, shining clean for the last time, and he was Lieutenant Janeway once more, with the commmendation letter from Winfield Scott fresh in his hand for the bastion he had enveloped without the loss of a man at Chapultepec. And he was Captain Janeway again, rallying Maxon's entire brigade, cooling it off, turning it about and leading it in personally through the gap in Pope's line to plug the hole.

"MacLaw," he said, "it's crazy, it's mad! But you'd better make it work! You'd better make it work! Because there isn't a chance left to me now! You've got your two companies! I'll do better for you than that! I'll give you a composite detail of sharpshooters and experts—all I've got —and a man to load for each rifleman. Mister O'Hirons! I'm pulling out of here at full dark. Pass the order to muffle all equipment. Butter the grease on wagon axles, thick! Cut ten wagons from the regimental trains and empty them. Double the loads on the others. Jettison what won't go on. Captain MacCluskey commands the composite detail. Pass the order. Get the covers off the civilian wagons as well—MacLaw," he said, "God bless you; you've brought back something in me I thought I'd lost forever. It's small return, but there's a brevet in it for you, if you pull this off, and finis for all of us, if you don't!"

The colonel put a fatigue party across the devastated area in close formation, picking up every piece of exploded brass, every recognizable fragment of an ammunition box. The brass he had dumped into the graves of the ten men of the guard detail, before he let the bodies be lowered in. The box fragments and what was left of the shattered wagons, he had stacked by the fires, for burning, through the night. So much for what the hostiles would find as evidence—unless they dug up the bodies of his men—but he had little hope that the sound of the explosions would not have carried the news back to the Indian camp. Little hope.

There was no hope at all in the doctor's mind, no chance that the hostiles would not know what those ten blurred explosive echoes meant to that column. They would have surged up from their fires, startled at the first distant roar, staring at one another in disbelief as the echoes continued, and then knowing. To-morow, with the dawn again, they would scout in slowly to try it out, to draw fire, and when they were sure that the bite was gone, they would gather in a vast circling horde and clamp down for the kill. And that's what the doctor wanted now, for it is a dreadful thing to see the pride and the power cut from under a regiment, leaving only the raw nerve net of what discipline it has, with only the sergeants to hold that net together.

While they closed the gap in the bivouac and called off the details for the move out, MacLaw went down to the sick wagons to tell the girl what he had to tell her. But when he found her, there was no need to tell her anything. She was waiting for him calm eyed, knowing the full import of what had happened and what was going to happen. She held out both her hands for his. "We will go, and you and the rear guard will stay. That's it, isn't it, Robert?"

"That is it, my dear," and because of the quiet courage he felt in her, he smiled. "Except that now, for a few moments, you will leave your patients and come with me," and he took her arm.

The Reverend Clutterhoe poked his scraggly head from the gap in the wagon cover, when the doctor rapped his knuckles on the tail gate. "Would you come out, Reverend? I have work for you."

Clutterhoe saw the girl then. "She must not come up here with us" he said. "No one from the sick wagons must come among us. Go," he said. "It is the will of the Lord!"

Doctor MacLaw reached up and clamped his fingers to Clutterhoe's wrist. "Step down, Reverend. I have scant knowledge of the will of God to-night, but I know my own. Marry us, Reverend. At once."

Clutterhoe objected, but his words soon faltered before MacLaw's insistence.

And so it was, under the great cathedral arch of the night sky, in the parish of the vast and opening west, with the music of the shattered bivouac about them, that those two were married. And when Clutterhoe's palsied voice had done with incantation, he wrote the certificate out with trembling fingers. "On this day, before me, an ordained minister of the Flock of the Heavenly Host, Martha Cutting, Spinster, and Robert MacLaw, a Doctor of Medicine, were married about twenty miles south and east of a place that is called the Mounds."

For honeymoon, the doctor and Martha walked back to the sick wagons hand in hand, without words.

They stood together for a few moments before he left her, with their hands still tight clasped. "Martha," he said. "No man ever knows his destiny, nor does a woman beyond the man she lives for. Some men live on the tops of lonely hills, some in towns in the valleys. Long years ago, something I could not understand sent me out to this country and here I will always stay.

Will you remember that—if it should come to pass that we never meet again on this earth? Once you have committed yourself to a course of life—do not ever turn back again."

"I know," she nodded. "There is no need to talk now. Hold me in your arms tightly now, for I shall need the strength of you for courage and the memory of your closeness for my guide lights."

CHAPTER TWELVE

H E KNELT DOWN beside Sergeant Elliott's blankets and the sergeant was out of them fast. "Yes, sir?"

"It's like this now," and MacLaw told him. And he said, "Our litter wounded goes on ahead in wagons with the main body. I want you to pass the word to the duty wounded that I'm relieving them this detail. That they may go on with the infantry. What do you suggest about the led horses?"

"No, sir. We better keep them damned led horses with us. May need 'em, sir. Besides nobody'd know how to talk to 'em. They got temperament bad. Bunch of theayter actors. Besides, one peep out of the trumpet and twenty miles away and they'll tear out of their halters and come back to the troop, sir. They ain't foolin'. They feel real bad."

"Keep them then."

"And the duty wounded, sir?"

"I covered that, sergeant. They may go with the main body."

"Yes, sir, but I wouldn't like to pass that order to D Troop—what with some infantry staying here. Nobody's bad hurt enough, that an order like that wouldn't make them much worse. Does the captain insist on it, sir?"

"Keep them with us," the doctor shrugged.

For a moment, Sergeant Elliott stood there in his underdrawers, just as he'd leaped from his blankets, but embarrassment twisted him now, like a stomach pain, and he could not talk of what was in his mind to say, for enlisted men think odd things of officers and an opinion grows fast and silently. They don't talk much, but it goes between the eyes and from the corners of eyes in formation, and it's as solid as a vote, with no vestige of sentiment unless it's questioned some night over the beer. And what a good officer is, no one will ever know well enough to say in words, for a lot of things go to make one up. And don't ever forget it, it's the men's reaction that does it in the end. Not words, not effort, but deep in the men's minds somewhere, they are for—or against. Either way, they'll perform still, for that's Army. But one way is beyond and above, and that way is rare.

They'd never liked Forsythe, for he was a gray man with no moisture left in him. They hadn't liked Captain Rogers, before Forsythe, because Rogers tried too hard and it showed. But through the long and bloody days from Cashman's something had grown in their minds about this doctor. So it doesn't say in the book to have a doctor command? So what do you care? Everything happens to D Troop. Take this, too. But now they *wanted* to take it. It was more than pay and get home. It was Cap'n MacLaw, and by God, it was Cap'n MacLaw! You wanta argue? And how can you know that sort of thing? Well, there is only one way, and it takes time. It takes ten years—fifteen maybe—and there's a man at the gate in civvies, rolling his hard hat in his hands and hating his necktie. "I heard the cap'n was living here, sir. Braunheimer, sir. D Troop, back on that Paradise march, maybe the cap'n remembers? Calling to pay my respects, sir. No think you, sir. I'm just passin' through town, but I just, I had—well, the cap'n—"

So, to help Elliott, Doctor MacLaw held out his soot smeared hand. "It is a pleasure to serve with you, Sergeant Elliott, and with D Troop," and for the first time in his life, Elliott blushed as their hands clasped. "That's it"—he bobbed his head—"what I had to say to the cap'n. And not only me. You'll get a good day's work out of all of us, sir. A good day's work."

They got the dummy wagon circle in position and let the campfires inside go down to eliminate silhouetting. MacCluskey manned the outguard line and set up his Cossack posts for the night. The colonel bled the main body out of camp, a company at a time, standing to watch each one pass, listening for metal clanks, for any sharp noises beyond the slow foot shuffle. All pails and lanterns were off the wagons, everything inside was muffled in wadded blankets. It made a hell of a noise close to, but there were no sharp sounds to carry far, and God must have turned his face upon them, for ten minutes before the tail cleared the circle, a blinding rain came in from the north and lashed the prairie for an hour, killing all sound but its driving fury.

It was as if the regiment and the civilian convoy had passed through a great door and the door had closed softly behind it. There is a shaft of loneliness that hits men's hearts and puts holes in them, for the outer winds to blow through. In the circle, men huddled together, hearing those winds and understanding them without words. Ninety-six of the regiment and thirty-one in D Troop, with the ten wagoners.

Fear crouches just beyond clear outline. It is gray, with a lacing of cold swamp green. And there is a smell to it that makes the nostrils rigid. But there is no working bravery, beyond anger and cussedness, for the job in hand. All else is insensitivity, that knows no fear. And a man without fear is a poor soldier, for he's only half a man.

After the main body was well away, they built up the fires into great smoke smudges with the rain soaked wood. There were few bird calls outside the circle that night, and concern was in the doctor that possibly it was too late, and that a hostile party had moved on ahead to the Mounds, to be in position before the march arrived. But when the rain cleared, the fire glow on the clouds was still there less than five miles behind, and as bright as it had been for the last four nights.

Then that rear guard knew for certain what would come to pass in the first half light of tomorrow's dawn. When the balance is tight drawn, and you can see the figures evened off on both bottom lines, the calmness of the inevitable comes upon you. A curtain drops tight across the back of your mind and nothing that happened before can come beyond it, for it can no longer have continuity with the rest of living. There is a humble consciousness at last, that no one man can be very important in this world beyond the daily work he does. And that humility walks you close to God at last. Then, in quiet and awful calmness, you hear God's footsteps soft beside you, and the tears well hot and desperate in your soul for all the years you have not listened. You are a child again in a heart that beats full in a man's body—and there is no meanness left upon you, no wilfulness, no false ambition and no pride. You have a sense only of time having run out, leaving behind it a consciousness of waste and unfulfillment, with no second chance now, ever to make it up. But a sense too, that that is living and that it is known in advance and understood. That all you are required to do is try, and fail, and try again. That is why you hear the footsteps, at last, and know within you that they have always been there, but that only now have you listened.

CHAPTER THIRTEEN

A LL EVENING, the Cossack posts watched the darkness beyond
the position and the wood details kept the fires bright. They
clattered pans and sang until Call to Quarters, and afterward,
every hour, the guard changed noisily in an outrageous panto-
mime of march and countermarch around the circle. Challenging
itself, halting, droning a repetition of General Orders, picking up
the empty show.

As the cold hours marched down the darkened world, the
men slept in sprawled exhaustion, but MacLaw and MacCluskey
sat close to their fire, their minds sixty-eight years in the future
and neither one of them knowing it.

The doctor said, "Things come to us from the past and we
accept them blindly as truth, but we are not meant to. We are
meant only to consider them for what worth they may have to
us in our time, to modify and reject them, if they are worthless as they stand. It is written in books, for instance, that great
care must be exercised in the diagnosis of smallpox, and that has
worth. But it is also written in books that generally speaking,
infantry must fight where it stands—and that is worthless!"

Charles Bancroft MacCluskey lay on his elbow, listening with
every fibre of consciousness, for there was a voice just behind
him that had spoken coldly to him earlier in the evening, and
the doctor's talk would keep it from speaking again. But deep
within him, MacCluskey knew that the other voice did not have
to speak again. "MacCluskey," it had said, "by sundown tomorrow you will be dead."

"Why should infantry march from A to B, if it has to fight at B?" the doctor asked. "Wagons could bring it to B, fresh and strong for the fight."

"Oh, nonsense," MacCluskey grinned, "you couldn't sell that to the generals in a thousand years. Infantry slogs on foot." But his mind was with his wife in St. Louis. *I hope Louise is having a pleasant evening. I hope there is music for her and amusing company and that she will sleep well and not worry about me, for she will need all her strength when the word comes.*

"But if the infantry can march in wagons," the doctor said, *"it can fight from wagons.* Indians have tactics, MacCluskey, and strategy. They have control in the field. Theirs is not a mad attack rush, hit or miss. For centuries they've held to the circling attack. The answer is: Break their circle!"

MacCluskey laughed. "If you value your commission, never put it in writing!" *I can't even write a letter to leave for Louise, for she must never know I saw this thing coming toward me.*

"Like this." the doctor's eyes were bright with enthusiasm. He broke a splinter in the firelight he traced a V in the dirt. "A chevron of wagons full of riflemen pointed toward their attack circle. Each wagon echeloned, so that it has a field of fire clear of the wagon in front. Mounted men riding with the lead wagon horses, so that the hostiles can't get at their heads and swerve them. The back of the V closed by other mounted men and the spare horses inside. And what have you got? *"You've got a moving fort!* Break through their circle with it, and stop till it forms again. Then break through again, each time it does form!"

Charles MacCluskey stared at the doctor in sudden gratefulness, for MacLaw's thinking took the insistence of the secret voice from his mind and bent his mind to his own considered wisdom of his trade. "You know what you are doing, don't you? You are putting an ax to the roots of modern military science," MacCluskey grinned. "You are denying the shibboleths of a thousand years and going back to scythe chariots. Good Lord, why not! Let's go on with it. It has always bothered me mightily that the flanks of a position should be so all-fired important. Since Cannae, every general in the world has worried himself sick about his flanks. But Ghengis Khan didn't! He denied his flanks, turned them in upon himself, refused them when they were threatened with envelopment."

"Of these things, I am not too well read," MacLaw told him, "but if you will take medicine as an example, the thinking and writing on the science is full of false trails and countermarching. But therein, any young doctor may discover the right pathway and point it out, whereas in the Army, the very essence of the service requires a junior to give silent lip-service to the views of a senior."

"Aren't you right!" MacCluskey laughed. "Has it ever occurred to you how ridiculous it really is, that artillery proceeds toward action with the gun barrels pointing in the opposite direction from which they will eventually shoot? As an infantryman, it always has to me. Arrived at the fight, with all the vulnerability ahead of you, that is, your horses and then your caisson of ammunition, you must unhook from the gun, gallop back the way you have come to cover, man handle the gun around until it points toward the enemy, then load and fire."

"How would you do it?"

Again MacCluskey laughed. "How did they do it with the ancient catapults? Ran them in on *four* wheels. But somebody years later decided that a gun should have only *two* wheels and a trail, so that it could be traversed easily and that is the way it has been ever since"—he pounded the ground with his fist—"and of course with only *two* wheels, the piece must be dragged by its trail, for if you dragged it by the barrel, it would overbalance and topple. Whereas the scientific answer is to put it on *four* wheels, muzzle front, and once on the battery position, remove two of the wheels for traversing. How many years do you think it will take before the brass think of that?"

Fire and maneuvre was what they talked—and they did not even know the meaning of the words. But as they sat there planning their signals for to-morrow and allocating the men to the wagons, the wagons by sections and the squads of D troop to fend each wagon, the memory of Appomattox and of Washita and of the Little Big Horn were already aging on the pages of a young country's history, and the still-blank pages ahead were rustling faintly for a future that would write St. Lô and Remagen and Bastogne upon them.

"It isn't Army," MacCluskey shook his head, "because it'll work!" *Louise must marry again. Oh, damn, damn!* "Guard relief," he said, and he got up. "What was your Class, MacLaw?" He looked at his silver watch. "The Old Man has got eight miles of distance behind him by now; maybe nine. Eighteen miles, he'll have by sun up. What'll we do—plan to hold the position until ten A.M., to give him time to dig? God, I'd hate to have eagles on my shoulders out there to-night."

Since the last counterattack that afternoon, before the fires came down once more, Holmes, Nethersmith and Corporal Fleming had been checked as "Missing in action." But at half past two A.M., Corporal Fleming rejoined the Troop. For eleven hours, he had crawled and hopped and rolled himself across the blackened waste, circling around the Indian camp, heading for the glow of the column's campfire, with his left Achilles' tendon severed, so that his foot hung like a chop on a string.

"The man said don't never miss reveille," he told Elliott. "Holmes and poor old Nethersmith don't draw pay no more."

They got him in blankets and poured whiskey into him. He almost tore the hands off Elliott while the doctor cut in and stitched the tendor. "It gonna work, cap'n?"

"If you work it, Fleming. There's an inch missing. How old are you?"

"Don't rightly know, sir. It says twenty-eight on the record. A pretty good guess."

"Like hell," Elliott told him. "You lied three years when you come in. You ain't twenty-five."

"It'll work then," MacLaw told him. "Youth makes everything work."

"Sergeant," Fleming grinned, "you're sore 'cause you gotta change the Morning Report! Ain't you ashamed?"

CHAPTER FOURTEEN

THE NIGHT wore itself down toward the new day. The stars went out, and gray light seemed to rise from the ground in sick miasma. There were a few moments hung in the void of time, when no shape was quite what it should be in fact—merely castoffs of the night itself, hulking, fragmented, threatening— then definition limned them into wagon covers and ammunition boxes, sleeping men rolled close together, the horse lines. Then the curtain rose cautiously, and the flat of the land commenced to draw out in extended panorama until the whole lonesome countryside spread in all directions in stark desolation, until you could see the coarse grass, blade for blade, and the glint on a worn horseshoe and the white eyeballs of the men.

An hour before the dawn, cautious reconnaissance groups came down upon the position, fending it widely, well beyond extreme range. By sun up, there was a great mass of hostiles forming to the south and east and about seven o'clock, they strung out in long, reaching lines to ride into their circling attack formation. When the position was completely ringed, small groups began to push in upon it, firing into it with screaming contempt. And presently they were thrusting in close enough for their fire to be returned, in spaced, aimed shots.

MacCluskey had the south sector, MacLaw the north. The infantry riflemen fired on prepared rests, with each man's loader behind him. The ammunition allocation to the infantry was eight hundred rounds with forty-eight men to fire. Eight hundred rounds to hold to ten o'clock—to get away with. There were three hundred and eighty rounds left, per carbine, in D Troop.

For an hour the hostiles came in sporadically, closer each time to draw a fire, but they drew no volume, and that was apparently all the confirmation of last night's explosions that they needed, for two hundred of them came all the way in about nine o'clock, as skirmishers in the approach and then bunching to break through into the north side of the circle. Aimed fire laid them across the middle distance, horse and man, until they bunched.

But when they bunched, their gods were in it and the impetus was gathered full—and a Plains Indian fights even after he's dead. They hit the outer lines and broke through like a flash flood from mountain rain. About two dozen made the break-through, with some of the ponies going down as they hit the barricade, catapulting their thrashing riders ahead of them for a close fight with knives, boots and clubbed rifles. Some of them jumped clean, and there were mounted Indians inside the circle, shrieking and pirouetting their ponies.

Those fights are so fast and so furious that it is impossible to see fully what you do see. But it all registers on the subconscious and it all comes back with the years of memory afterwards. Maslin of D Troop with a steel pipe axe sunk into his shoulder at the neck, and the blood pumping into the air in quick jets, with the brave who had done for him being pulled off his mount and clubbed and kicked halfway across the circle to the picket lines until his head hung loose like a knot in a wet towel. The men on the far side broke out of position to run down the foray, firing cross fire, bulldogging the ponies with dirty hands twisted into the head thongs.

It broke into a dozen scattered fights, with the fury of a thousand years. The picket line horses screamed and thrashed in panic, and the ululation of the war cries knifed through the confusion like the shrieks of beasts in agony.

There was no order to it, no pattern; it was a torn fabric of racing shadows, red and vibrant in the morning light with the savage quality of a mad dance. Men kill in two ways: cold, steady with intense concentration on the business, and again, hot with primeval savagery. There is an uncleanliness to it so shocking, that the mind turns in perspective and casts off all templates of civilization, denies them utterly in its own defense, and suddenly sees the thing as its own justification, with its own right to outrageous beauty. The years go out the window, and men live on instinct alone and the stark remembrance of the slime that gave them instinct.

For there was necessity to kill them all, so that none might get back to their main body with the word that the circle was loosely held and the bulk of the enemy had gone. So they killed them all, and all of it was over in seven minutes that would remain as a lifetime in memory. They plugged the break in the barricade and stood-to, breathless and white-eyed, for the next attack. There were six infantrymen dead with Maslin, and four of them wounded, and Reinecke's elbow cut clean out of his arm.

MacCluskey came over to the doctor, looking at his watch. "This we can't take, MacLaw. If they keep coming in on us this way, they'll chop us to a nub. The circle is too big to stop them. We haven't enough men."

"I don't intend to take it again."

The doctor climbed up on a wagon box and put his glasses on the north. No dust. The main body had thirteen hours of time. That looked like the deal. "What do you think, MacCluskey?"

"I think if they break us again, we're for it. That's where we can't take it. We're sitting ducks after they close the range. Take a look! They're massing again to the west. Let's put the show on the road!"

The doctor got the ten wagons marshaled in a chevron formation, the drivers lying flat at the reins between oat sacks, two troopers right and left of the lead wagon horses, five riflemen and five loaders in each stripping wagon box and the rest of D Troop closing the rear of the V. That way they had an all around field of fire, rolling or standing still.

"They'll give way," the doctor shouted through his cupped hands to the men, "when we hit their circle. They always do! The flanks of the break will circle back on themselves and bunch! Pour the soup to them then! But keep going beyond until you get the Halt from me! Stop then, and let them reform in a circle again! And again we'll break it! You've got something over twenty miles to go in three mile spurts! On the trumpet now. Trumpeter, give me the regimental preface on all calls. The troopers know the calls; the wagoners will draw up when the lead troopers signal them to stop. Prepare to mount!"

And some doughfoot yelled across to another, "Leave us know how it all comes out, Ballard! Write us a postcard!"

"Mount!" The doctor waved to MacCluskey and drew off to the head of the V, with Waller, the trumpeter riding close to him. The galloping hostile circle was five hundred yards out beyond the dummy wagon ring, and the assault group to the westward was gathering to ride in. "Trumpeter, give me Forward and kick trot on the end of it." Waller flicked his C horn up with a parade flourish, snapped it to his lips, and the horn six-noted Regiment, then Forward, Trot in a rollicking brass scream.

They burst out of the defense position at full gallop to the north in a cloud of black cindery dust, heading straight for the circling hostiles, and tearing a two-hundred-yard gap through them before they could get back on balance, tearing the gap with murderous close-in fire, and lashing the recoiling flanks as they went through.

The secret of it was its simplicity and the horse sense that prompted the doctor to explain it to everyone. The waggoners guided on each other on each arm of the chevron, each man holding his galloping team in the protection of the off rear side of the wagon ahead, so that no wagon masked the fire of any other. And the leading wagons had an unobstructed field of fire straight ahead as well as to the side. As each wagon tore through the widening gap, its fire power came to bear until the destruction of that first breakthrough was unbelievable. The recoiling Indians fouled each other, bunched into close-range targets, and went down in heaps of thrashing mounts. The surprise of it reduced it to mass murder.

They kept on going for a mile beyond, until the doctor had the trumpeter draw them down to a walk. But at the walk, they kept going still while the whole Indian mass behind them bunched and palavered, and the west flank foray, not seeing the breakout, tore through the dummy wagon circle and drew up in baffled consternation.

The sub-chiefs called in their people. The mass broke up into small, gesticulating groups, arguing in confusion, staring after the slow moving wagons, trying to beat down the spectre in their minds of this new thing they had failed to cope with, that had left them completely off balance, and shaken with loss of face. Then the individual groups came together, and the coalition of tribes massed once more in powwow that had no unity beyond frustration and anger, no stimulus to action beyond the sight of the chevroned wagons still moving slowly away from them toward the north in a low cloud of dust.

There was contempt in the very slowness of the movement and a challenge to pursue that they could not deny. But there was fear in the Indians at the sudden and awful havoc they had suffered—and fear breeds caution.

It was almost half an hour before lines of horsemen began to string out on either side again and gallop in pursuit, for a thousand years of tactical thinking was gone like the snows of winter. But when they came, they came. Like thunder down the wind. That's when the doctor halted full, to rest the horses and wait.

He waited with each wagon of riflemen in mutual fire support of every other wagon. He watered the horses sparsely. He held his fire.

The long lines of horsemen passed him and closed in front of the wagons and went once more into the attack circle, ringing him round and tightening the noose. But the doctor didn't let them close the range. He had three miles behind him and a half hour's rest. When they began to bunch for a charge again, he waited until the dust plumes of their sporadic fire began to fly twenty yards from the wagon chevron; then he started off again.

The show rolled and the dust behind it masked the rolling when Waller the trumpeter lipped it into Gallop. And again they hit the amazed circle, tore a gap through it, cut down the recoiling shoulders of the penetration and got a mile beyond it.

That time the hostiles reformed quickly and came after them close onto their rear. So close that the last two wagons were knocking them off like pigeons, until they drew back out of range.

The Indians kept on doing what they had always done, but they weren't happy, for they had never drawn qualified fire from moving wagons before, and it cost them plenty. With disorganized desperation, they began to put on sporadic attacks, with no over-all control, the tribes and sub-tribes breaking into small fanatical groups, and attempting to cut into the chevron by sheer force of a will to do it or die trying.

It wasn't their way of fighting, but by its sheer unreasoned fury it almost worked, for what it amounted to was a swift attack on the chevron's point, and as soon as a nearby group saw that attack underway, they would dash in at their angle and hit one of the arms. Then a third group would hit the opposite side and a fourth would strike at the tail. This tactic shifted the fire from the wagons in all directions, shifted the concentration, but it also did what Janeway had feared in his own command when he divided it. It allowed each attack to be met as it came in with the full force of the defending fire and driven off. It threatened the tribes with piecemeal defeat.

They seemed to realize this, at the same time they realized they couldn't get in to tear the wagons apart, ride them off separately for the overturn and slaughter. So they went back to circling, but again the wagons wouldn't stay inside their circle. They weren't happy, but they started at ten to one and they kept at it, because their minds weren't capable of doing anything else. Their dead and broken lay sprawled across the prairie for nine miles behind them, and still they kept on.

The doctor wasn't scot free, but every time they closed the circle, he broke it. And he kept on.

By three o'clock seven of his wagon horses lay out behind him, cut free of harness and shot by the outriding troopers, replaced in rope-mended harness by the spare horses. Crawford, Jones, Marcus and Kelly were off the troop rolls for keeps and there were nine dead riflemen in the wagons and two dying, with Captain MacCluskey shot through the lungs.

But the doctor kept going. Breaking the circle and riding north. Halting to rest the animals, letting the circle reform. Breaking it again.

Colonel Janeway, with his regiment deployed across the two moraines that the Cheyenne call Woman-that-Sleeps, saw the dust clouds at three o'clock. By four, he had the spectacle in his glasses, so he could watch the details of it. He saw the wagon V cut through, saw it stop beyond the open gap and go into all-around defense to wait for the futile circle to reform upon it, and a great flood of anger strangled him, for the thing was too outrageous to fit his experience. It was insane and an insult to tactical tradition. "That damned fool MacLaw is fighting his wagons instead of running away in them!" But young O'Hirons stood watching it with his mouth open, with belief full upon him in spite of his careful schooling.

"That's just what he is doing, sir," O'Hirons grinned. "Fighting them like Billy-be-damned! He's got a war on wheels, and it's working!" Then he saw Colonel Janeway's face and he wiped off his grin and exultation and said. "Yes, sir" solemnly.

Janeway spat. "War is not a playing field's game; it's a god-damned serious business, and it's got small place in it for the loose and harebrained gamble that isn't based on the sound rules of past experience. This thing you're looking at violates all the rules, and even if it works, it's wrong!"

O'Hirons stared at the colonel. "Yes, sir," he said, "even if it works."

Then the colonel narrowed his eyes and looked full into O'Hiron's young face. "And remember this too, mister," he said. "The business of being a professional soldier is just as cut and dried as fighting a war. When you're young, dry up your brain with the discipline imposed upon you by your lack of seniority, so that when you are old you've ruined all chance of ever getting an original idea again." He kept staring at O'Hirons for a long moment after he had said it, then he spat again and opened his eyes wide. "That way," he said, "you get to be a general. Looks to me from here like MacLaw has cut the hostile force down badly. Looks about half strength from what it has been. Hate to take a battle away from a man, but I want you to switch the positions of the right and left flank companies. Move them forward, so when he's ready to make his final run for it, he can cut in under their covering fire."

"Yes, sir—and—"

"I know, boy. Very well. Pick whichever company you think's likely, and stay with it for your own piece of the fight. Never saw an adjutant yet who didn't think he wanted to fight. Nor had an adjutant I couldn't get along without. Go on out with them and cut yourself a piece of glory."

By five o'clock the doctor's mad caravan broke a circle of hostiles so close in to the Mounds that he kept on going until he was almost under supporting fire from Colonel Janeway's dug-in position on top. He had to keep going, for that last breakout took the last of the vinegar from him. There were nine wagon horses gone now and only two rifles still firing in each of the rear wagons as the fight wore down. He was in his own saddle only because shock was delayed from the cut across his left side and the inside of his left upper arm, torn wide. But an action will change, and when it does, the change comes fast. First Bull Run changed its color in less than twelve minutes. And that action changed faster. Suddenly the hostile attack circle that was forming slowed to an exhausted walk, like water in an arroyo that trickles down to a shallow flow and seeps out of sight in the sand. There were great gaps in the half formed circle, and it was thin as a worn-through pair of pants. The power of the tribes was bled white, and they knew it in the stoic fatalism that was half of their savage way of life. As they slowed, a group of Cheyennes, in closer than the rest, came down on the forward position of the two flank companies and the word passed sharp to open fire. The infantry rifles blazed by volley and, Mr. O'Hirons with C Company saw a brown hip bone dead in the sights of his borrowed rifle. He drew in his breath and squeezed off at the word, and saw the hip bone smear crimson, saw his duck crash off the pony and strike the ground like a sack of meal. He fired again and smashed the Cheyenne's face. He felt better.

The ragged circle wavered. It straggled to a halt. It bunched into querulous subtribes and then, like the glory of other days, it faded and was gone.

That, in itself, is unbelievably shocking. You can't bring it into mental focus until hysteria lashes you into the knowledge that a fight is won. It cannot be that one hundred and thirty-seven men have crushed a thousand, torn the heart from hostile pride and sent it scurrying from a lost field in frantic, panic-ridden tatters.

The doctor got down from his pumped horse and wrapped the last of his shirt around his arm, drawing it tight. The men in the wagons climbed out, and suddenly Sergeant Elliott, still sitting his horse in utter weariness on the shoulder of the knoll, raised his hat and pointed to the southwest. "God bless, sir, the main Indian encampment didn't move today! No dust!"

The doctor climbed to a wagon box and put his glasses on the twenty miles they had come, and there was no thick corded dust back there nor anywhere on the horizon, except from the scattered tribesmen. He stepped down again and stood quite still, casing his glasses. The field of the last close fight lay sprawled about him just under the Mounds, but the hot pursuit was ended. For thirteen days it had closed in on the column's tail, ruthless and inexorable, and to have the threat of it lifted now was more unbelievable than today's business. Why? But to hell with why, for the road was open to the Paradise and General Cook, and that's all that counts. That's the mission.

Men stared at each other in amazement and looked back, their eyes shaded with their hats. On the Mounds above, Janeway's men cheered and came out of their rifle pits. But back there, where it had stopped last night, that great threatening movement was still stopped.

The doctor walked slowly across to look at Captain MacCluskey. The bullet had gone through his chest sideways and opened the cavity twice to the outer air. The blood bubbled at the lips of the wounds, and MacCluskey's chest whispered softly with the labor of his collapsing lungs. His eyes moved slightly to MacLaw's face, but he could no longer speak. MacLaw had seen it many times, but it was always something that stifled him inside.

He knelt down and took MacCluskey's hand in both of his, and he watched the captain's face for fear. Men die in many ways. There is a calmness in some of them after the first rebellion, a deep sense of inevitability that allows them to accept the transition with all the dignity of their souls. That calmness was on McCluskey and there was no place left for fear.

Finally, the doctor climbed down from the wagon.

The Pawnee flung headlong and jammed between the wheel spokes of McCluskey's wagon was dead, too. Doctor MacLaw grabbed his scabbed and greasy heels and pulled his head and arms free of the wheel. Then he stared at the face, twisted, in war paint, and he knelt quickly for a closer professional examination. He went over the dead brave's arms and hands and the upper part of his grease-slimed body. He tore a rag from his tattered shirt, soaked it down with the last of his canteen water, and scrubbed the paint from the cooling flesh.

Then he expelled air between his teeth in a long whistling sound and threw the sodden rag from him. He stood up with the laughter tearing at his diaphragm, and his face twisted between shock and tears.

"Is the captain all right?" Sergeant Elliott stepped toward him quickly and put a hand to his arm. MacLaw stared at him and then started to laugh.

"Take it easy, sir!" the Sergeant said. "It's like that sometimes. You can crack wide open with it. Don't let go."

Then MacLaw pulled himself together and shook his head. "It is never the crises, Elliott—the climaxes—it's what comes afterwards!"

On the mound top, he went at once to Martha. She was standing at the great wheel of a wagon, calling to him, "We have it! We have the rash! Raised red papules late last night, spreading into hemispheroids, filled with clear serum!"

"I know," he said. "I have just seen it," and he pointed to the dead Indian below. A man near Martha roared with laughter, slapping his corduroyed thigh with the sound of wood on wood. "Dang that Tyler Clutterhoe! And he'll take all the credit! But how'll he account to God for the souls of Lettie and Garsten Ott?"

CHAPTER FIFTEEN

COLONEL JANEWAY was livid when the doctor saw him. "You blithering fool!" he roared. "You fought those wagons! They were your getaway vehicles! If you'd told me this last night, I wouldn't have agreed to it! It's tactical suicide, what you've done! My God, man, you've won a fabulous battle, *but it can't be done that way!*"

"Yes, sir," the doctor said, "but it's much worse than that. You remember telling me that in all your forty-two years in the Army you had always expected the worst, and only been disappointed twice? Well, I'm afraid I bring you your third disappointment, sir. You haven't got smallpox in this column at all. You've got chickenpox."

The colonel was on his feet. He stared at MacLaw and the quick blood of his anger washed furiously into his head until his eyes distended and became blind with it for a second of speechless fury. "Mister O'Hirons!" he yelled. "Send that slab-bottomed Prussian quack to me," and to Haberschaft he bellowed, "Blast your eyes! You've got chickenpox, not small-pox, you blabbermouth. Get down and see for yourself! Get it through your thick Dutch skull, and spread the good word to the command at once! God's teeth"—the Colonel flung up both arms—"chickenpox!" Then, with the blood roaring in his brain, he whipped around on MacLaw. "How the hell do you know it's chickenpox?"

"I am not a cavalry officer," MacLaw said, "I am a doctor of medicine."

The colonel stared in utter horror, and the blood let go and he went down under it as if it had been a clubbed rifle. He lived twenty years longer, but he never quite recovered from that unspeakable breach of Army Regulations.

The doctor stood looking at Martha, his hat in hand. "Red dolls," he said, "and paper pinwheels since the second day out of Cashman's. Hand mirrors and combs, you scattered in our trail!"

"I didn't scatter them in our trail, I scattered them beside the trail," she said. "So the rear battalion wouldn't march through it. It was the only weapon I had, so I used it. The debris of the sick wagons, with every bright bauble I could contaminate and add to it. You have not violated your oath of Hippocrates, and I wish it had been smallpox!"

The doctor frowned. "They couldn't move camp today, because the squaws and children are rotten with it." He rubbed a hand across his chin. "Almost two weeks, for our people to come down with it, but the Indians have no immunity to white men's diseases. So it hit them a day ahead."

"I fought by your side," she said fiercely, "and a woman is free to use any weapon she chooses!"

Then for the first time in many days he roared with laughter, and he put his hands to her shoulders and folded her into his arms. "Martha—Martha—'and the squaws I am told are more savage than the men.' " And then the laughter died within him and he straightened his arms, holding her from him so that he could look into her face full. "Martha, there will not be a sense of second best in you, will there? Of another having walked in the rooms of the house that should be yours alone?"

For a moment she stood looking at him in silence, then she closed her eyes and shook her head violently. "Never, Robert, for you have kept your house beautifully, and you do me great honor in letting me live in it! And now will you sit down and let me bandage that arm properly!"

You got ten dollars extra pay a month in those days, for commanding. General Cook's paymaster gave the doctor a five-dollar gold piece for his fifteen days. They never got around to calling that town in Wyoming, "Clutterhoe." The historical society's sign on State Highway 55 says it was named for a woman called Martha MacLaw who prevented the tribes from the Wind River reservations from joining Sitting Bull, but it doesn't say how she did it, for people forget the details of those things. It says: "MACLAW, WYOMING. ROTARY, WEDNESDAYS, 12 O'CLOCK. KLEINBEIN HOTEL."

But take U. S. 1 out of Baltimore, if you want the story. Fifteen miles brings you to the fort gates. That cavalry regiment is stationed there now with—Armored, light—after its designation. Drive up past the D Troop day room and the tank parks and you come to regimental headquarters. They have the battle honors in the Old Man's office. From Chapultepec to the Great Wagon Fight, Wyoming 1876, through to Bastogne and Czechoslovakia. They've got pictures of all the old regimental commanders—with George Patton's among them—and "Chick" Sheldon's will be there by now.

They'll show you the old trumpets and the older flags and the old handwritten morning reports, for so much is cavalry courtesy. But if they really like you, they'll take you over to the club for a drink and they'll say, "Horses? Oh, to hell with horses! You think there's something unromantic about tanks? Something newfangled? Not in this regiment. We invented them seventy years ago out West." And they'll grin at the youngster who commands D Troop, and they'll say, "Tell him about Captain MacLaw—Doctor."

THE END

Printed in Great Britain
by Amazon

79283061R00075